THE BRAVE FREE MEN

The Roguskhoi stood at one end of the melon field, glowering toward the shields of the militia. The four Roguskhoi chieftains stood to the side, distinguished from the ordinary warriors by black leather neckbands supporting bibs of chain mail. They seemed older than the troopers; their skin showed duller and darker; flaps of skin or muscle, like wattles, grew under their chins. They watched the advancing militia in mild perplexity, then uttered a set of harsh sounds; the four companies moved forward at a passionless trot. From the militia came a thin sound, and the shields quivered. The Brave Free Men behind gave hoarse shouts and the militia steadied. At a distance of a hundred yards the Roguskhoi halted and brought their scimitars down, around, and back; their muscular processes knotted and tensed. In this position the Roguskhoi were a fearsome sight. The line of the militia sagged; some reflexively hurled their grenades, which exploded halfway between the lines. Shields on the left wing sagged, leaving the Brave Free Men without protection. For a half a second they hesitated, then charged, plunging against the instant hail of scimitars.

Also by the same author,
and available in Coronet Books:

The Anome
The Asutra

The Brave Free Men

Durdane Book 2

Jack Vance

CORONET BOOKS
Hodder Paperbacks Limited, London

Copyright © 1972 by Jack Vance

First published in Great Britain by
Coronet Books 1975

Printed and bound in Great Britain for
Coronet Books, Hodder Paperbacks Limited,
St. Paul's House, Warwick Lane,
London, EC4P 4AH
By C. Nicholls & Company Ltd.,
The Philips Park Press, Manchester

ISBN 0 340 19828 1

CHAPTER ONE

In a chamber high under the dormers of Fontenay's Inn, Etzwane stirred on his couch. He had slept but little. Presently he arose and went to the window, where the stars had paled on the violet dawn. The far slopes of the Ushkadel showed only the occasional green sparkle of a street lamp; the Aesthete palaces were dark.

In one of these palaces, thought Etzwane, the Faceless Man had slept no better than himself.

He turned away from the window and went to the washstand. A carbon-fume mirror gave back his image, a face altered both by the gloom of dawn and the umbral quality of the mirror. Etzwane peered close. This unreal, somewhat menacing person might well be himself most truly: the face sardonic, drooping of mouth, hollow of cheek; the skin sallow with a leaden sheen; the eyes dark holes, punctuated by a pair of glittering reflections. He thought: here stands Gastel Etzwane, first Chilite Pure Boy, then Pink-Black-Azure-Deep Greener, now a man of enormous power. He spoke to the image: "Today is a day of important events; Gastel Etzwane must not allow himself to be killed." The image gave back no reassurance.

He dressed and went down to the street. At a booth on the riverbank he ate fried fish and bread and considered his prospects for the day.

In broad essence the job was simple. He must go to Sershan Palace and there compel Sajarano, the Anome of Shant, to do his bidding. If Sajarano demurred, Etzwane need merely press a button to explode his head, for now Sajarano wore a torc and Etzwane did not. It was work of stark and brutal simplicity – unless Sajarano divined his solitary condition, his lack of ally or confederate, in which case Etzwane's situation became precarious.

With his breakfast finished there was nothing to deter him; he set forth up Galias Avenue. Sajarano, he reflected, would desperately be seeking to escape from his intolerable predicament. Etzwane asked himself: what, in Sajarano's place, would be his own response? Flight? Etzwane stopped short. Here was a contingency he had not considered. From his pouch he brought the pulse-emitter, once Sajarano's basic tool of law enforcement. Etzwane encoded the colours of Sajarano's torc. The yellow button would now – if necessary – detonate the torc, thereby removing Sajarano's head. Etzwane pushed the red "Seek" button. The box hummed, the sound fluctuating with change of direction. At maximum the box pointed towards Sershan Palace. Etzwane proceeded, more thoughtful than ever. Sajarano had not taken to flight. He might have evolved a strategy more active.

Galias Avenue terminated at the Marmione Plaza, where a fountain of milk-white water played over artifacts of purple glass; the Koronakhe Steps opposite, constructed by King Caspar Pandamon, rose towards the terraces of the Ushkadel. At the Middle Way Etzwane left the steps and proceeded eastwards, around the sweep of the Ushkadel. The prismatic Palace Xhiallinen rose above him; here lived Jurjin, the Faceless Man's "Benevolence." Among a dozen other mysteries, this: why had Sarajano

6

selected so conspicuously beautiful a girl for his deputy?
... The mystery, in this case, might be more apparent
than real, so Etzwane speculated. The Anome, like any
man, could suffer the pangs of love. Jurjin of Xhiallinen
perhaps had reacted coolly to the attentions of Sajarano,
who was neither handsome, dashing, nor distinguished.
Perhaps she wondered when the Faceless Man had ordered her into his service and commanded her to take no
lovers. In due course the Faceless Man might have ordered her to look kindly upon Sarajano. So Etzwane con-
jectured.... He came to the Palace Sershan, neither more
nor less splendid than any of the others. Etzwane halted,
to review all circumstances. The next half-hour would de-
termine the future of Shant; each minute carried more
weight than all the days of a normal man's life. He looked
up and down the façade of Sershan Palace. Columns of
crystal, more lucid and transparent than air itself, frac-
tured the beams of the triple suns; the violet and green
domes beyond sheltered chambers where sixty Sershan
generations had lived, celebrated their festivals, and died.

Etzwane trudged forward. He crossed the loggia, approached the portico, and here he paused. Six doors of
inch-thick glass, each fifteen feet high, barred his way.
No light or movement appeared within. Etzwane hesitated, uncertain how to proceed. He began to feel foolish,
hence angry. He rapped on the glass. His bare knuckles
made little noise; he pounded with his fist. He saw movement within; a moment later a man came around the side
of the place. It was Sajarano himself.

"These are ceremonial doors," said Sajarano in a mild
voice. "We seldom open them; would you come this way?"

In glum silence Etzwane followed Sajarano to a side
entrance. Sajarano motioned him within. Etzwane halted

and searched Sajarano's face, to which Sajarano returned a faint smile, as if he found Etzwane's wariness amusing. With his hand on the yellow button Etzwane entered the palace.

"I have been expecting you," said Sajarano. "Have you breakfasted? Perhaps you'll take a cup of tea. Shall we go up to the morning room?"

He led the way to a sunny chamber with a floor of green and white jade tiles. The wall to the left was shrouded in dark green vines; the wall to the right was clear white alabaster. Sajarano motioned Etzwane to a wicker chair beside a wicker table, then at a sideboard served himself a few morsels of food and poured tea into a pair of silverwood cups.

Etzwane carefully seated himself; Sarajano took the chair opposite, his back to the ceiling-high windows. Etzwane studied him with sombre calculation, and Sajarano once again gave back his faint smile. Sajarno was not an imposing man physically; his features were small; under a broad high forehead his nose and mouth seemed almost immature, his chin was a nubbin. The Anome of popular conception was vastly different from this mild, reasonable man.

Sajarano sipped his tea. Best to take the initiative, thought Etzwane. He spoke in a careful monotone: "As I previously mentioned, I represent that segment of the public which is seriously concerned in regard to the Roguskhoi. We believe that if decisive steps are not taken, in five years there will be no more Shant – only a great horde of Roguskhoi. As the Anome it is your duty to destroy these creatures; such is the trust the people of Shant repose in you."

Sajarano nodded without emphasis and sipped his tea.

Etzwane left his cup untouched. "These considerations," Etzwane continued, "forced my friends and myself to extreme lengths, as you know."

Sajarano nodded once more: a kindly reassuring nod. "These friends: who are they?"

"Certain persons who are shocked by the acts of the Roguskhoi."

"I see. And your position: you are the leader?"

"I?" Etzwane gave an incredulous laugh. "By no means."

Sajarano frowned. "Would it be fair to assume that the others of your group are known personally to me?"

"It is a matter which really has no bearing on the issue," said Etzwane.

"Perhaps not, except that I like to know with whom I am dealing."

"You need deal with no one; you need only muster an army and drive the Roguskhoi back into Palasedra."

"You make it sound so simple," said Sajarano. "A further question: Jurjin of Xhiallinen spoke of a certain Ifness, who demonstrated remarkable abilities. I confess to curiosity regarding this Ifness."

"Ifness is a remarkable man indeed," said Etzwane. "As to the Roguskhoi: what do you propose to do?"

Sajarano ate a slice of fruit. "I have considered the matter carefully, to this effect. The Anome is what he is only because he controls the lives of all the people of Shant but is himself exempt from such control. This is the definition of the Anome. It no longer defines me; I wear a torc. I can take no responsibility for acts or policies not my own. In short I propose to do nothing."

"Nothing whatever? What of your normal duties?"

"I resign them all to you and your group. You wield the

power; you must bear the burdens." Sajarano laughed at Etzwane's glum expression. "Why should I go into a hysteria of effort over policies whose wisdom I doubt? What nonsense this would be!"

"Am I to understand that you no longer consider yourself Anome?"

"That is correct. The Anome must work anonymously. I can no longer do this. You, Jurjin of Xhiallinen, others in your group know my identity. I am no longer effective."

"Then who is to be Anome?"

Sajarano shrugged. "You, your friend Ifness, another member of your group. You control the power, you must accept the responsibility."

Etzwane frowned. Here was a contingency for which he had not prepared. Obduracy, threats, scorn, anger: yes. Supine relinquishment: no. It was too easy. Etzwane became wary, Sajarano's subtlety far exceeded his own. He asked cautiously, "You will cooperate with us?"

"I will obey your orders, certainly."

"Very well. First, a state of national emergency is to be proclaimed. We will identify the danger, then make it clear that an effort of major proportions must be made."

Sajarano made a polite sound. "So much is easy. Remember, however, that the population of Shant is over thirty million souls; to cry emergency to so many is a serious affair."

"Agreed; no dispute here whatever. Second, women must be evacuated from all areas adjacent to the Wildlands."

Sajarano gave him a look of polite bewilderment. "Evacuated to where?"

"To the coastal cantons."

Sajarano pursed his small mouth. "It is not all so simple. Where will they live? Will their children accompany them? What of their homes, their ordinary duties? The cantons affected would number twenty or thirty. That is a large number of women."

"Which is precisely why we want them moved," said Etzwane. "That number of women impregnated by Roguskhoi means a vast horde of Roguskhoi!"

Sajarano shrugged. "What of the other difficulties I mentioned? They are real."

"Administrative detail," said Etzwane.

"To be handled by whom? Me? You? Your group?" Sarajano's tone had become patronizing. "You must think in terms of practicalities."

His strategy becomes clear, thought Etzwane. He will not oppose, but he will not help, and will do all in his power to induce indecision.

"Third," said Etzwane, "the Anome by executive order, must call into being a national militia."

Etzwane politely waited for Sajarano's objections; Sajarano did not disappoint him. "I regret the role of the carper, the defeatist; nevertheless I must point out that it is one matter to issue fiats; it is quite another to implement them. I doubt if you realize the full complexity of Shant. There are sixty-two cantons with nothing in common but language."

"Not to mention music and colour-lore.* Additionally, every citizen of Shant, with the seeming exception of yourself, hates and fears the Roguskhoi. The cantons are more united than you think."

Sajarano gave his little finger an annoyed jerk. "Let me

*Ael'skian: More exactly, the symbology of colour and colour-combinations; in Shant an intensely meaningful aspect of life, adding another dimension to perception.

11

recite the difficulties; perhaps then you will understand why I have drawn back from an intolerable confusion. To integrate sixty-two distinct militias, with sixty-two versions of life itself, is a stupendous task. An experienced staff is necessary. There is only myself and my single Benevolence – a girl."

"Since you consider my proposals inept," said Etzwane, "what were your own plans?"

"I have learned," said Sajarano, "that not every problem requires a solution. Many apparently urgent dilemmas dwindle and disappear if ignored. . . . Will you drink more tea?"

Etzwane, who had drunk no tea, signalled in the negative.

Sajarano leaned back in his chair. He spoke in a reflective voice: "The army you propose is impractical for yet another reason – perhaps the most cogent of all. It would be futile."

"Why do you say that?"

"It is really obvious. When any problem must be solved, when some irksome duty must be performed, it is referred to the Faceless Man. When folk complain of the Roguskhoi – have you heard them? – they always call on the Faceless Man to act! As if the Anome need only issue an ordinance to abate all and any nuisances! He has maintained peace for two thousand years, but it is the peace of a father upon a household of children."

Etzwane was silent for a period. Sajarano watched him with peculiar intensity. His gaze dropped to Etzwane's cup of tea. An idle thought drifted into Etzwane's head, which he rejected; certainly Sajarano would not attempt to poison him.

Etzwane said, "Your opinions are interesting, but they

argue only for passivity. My group insists that definite steps be taken: first, a declaration of national emergency; second, women must be evacuated from regions surrounding the Hwan; third, each canton must mobilize and train a militia; fourth, you must designate me as your Executive Aide, with all the authority you yourself command. If you are finished with your breakfast, we will issue these proclamations now."

"What if I refuse?"

Etzwane brought out the metal box. "I will take your head."

Sajarno nibbled at a wafer. "Your arguments are convincing." He sipped his tea and indicated Etzwane's cup. "Have you tasted it? I grow it at my own plantation."

Etzwane pushed his cup across the table. "Drink it."

Sajarano raised his eyebrows. "But I have my own cup."

"Drink it," said Etzwane in a harsh voice. "Otherwise I will believe that you have tried to drug me."

"Would I attempt so banal a ploy?" demanded Sajarano in a brassy voice.

"If you believed that I would discount such a trick as banal, then it becomes subtle. You can refute me by drinking."

"I refuse to be hectored!" spat Sajarano. He tapped his finger on the table. From the corner of his eye Etzwane saw the dark green ivy tremble; he glimpsed a glinting trifle and jerked back. From his sleeve he brought the broad-impulse tube he had taken from Sajarano and pointed it at the ivy. Sajarano emitted a terrible screech; Etzwane pushed the button. From behind the ivy sounded an explosion. Sajarano sprang across the table at Etzwane. "Murderer, murderer! Oh, the horror, the murder, the blood of my dear one!"

Etzwane struck Sajarano with his fist; Sajarano fell to the rug and lay moaning. From under the ivy a red puddle began to well out across the jade.

Etzwane fought to control his stomach. His mind twisted and reeled. He kicked Sajarano, who looked up with a yellow face and a wet mouth. "Get up!" cried Etzwane hoarsely. "If Jurjin is dead, the fault is yours; you are her murderer! You are my mother's murderer as well; if you had controlled the Roguskhoi long ago, there would not be this trouble!" He kicked Sajarano again. "Get up! Or I take your head in the bargain!"

Sajarano uttered a sob and staggered to his feet.

"So you instructed Jurjin to stand behind the ivy and kill me at your signal!" said Etzwane grimly.

"No, no! She carried an impulse gun, to drug you."

"You are insane! Can you imagine I would not have taken your head? And the tea – poisoned?"

"A soporific."

"What purpose does drugging me serve? Answer!"

Sajarano only shook his head. He had totally lost his poise; he pounded his forehead as if to subdue his thoughts.

Etzwane shook his shoulder. "What do you gain by drugging me? My friends would kill you!"

Sajarano mumbled, "I act as my inner soul dictates."

"From now on I am your inner soul! Take me to your office. I must learn how to communicate with the Discriminators* and the cantonal governments."

Sajarano, round shoulders slumping, led the way

*Avistïoi (literally *Nice Discriminators*): the constabulary of the Garwiy Aesthetic Corporation, and the single sophisticated police force of Shant.

through his private study to a locked door. He touched code-keys to open the door; they climbed a spiral staircase to a chamber overlooking all Garwiy.

A bench along the far wall supported a number of glass boxes. Sajarano made a vague gesture. "This is radio equipment. It sends a narrow beam to a relay station on top the Ushkadel, and cannot be tracked. I press this button to transmit messages to the Office of Proclamations; by this, to the Chief Discriminator; by this, to the Hall of Cantons; by this, to the Office of Petitions. My voice is disguised by a filtering device."

"What if I were to speak?" asked Etzwane. "Would anyone know the difference?"

Sajarano winced. His eyes were dull with pain. "No one would know. Do you plan to become Anome?"

"I have no such inclination," said Etzwane.

"In effect this is the case. I refuse all further responsibility."

"How do you answer the petitions?"

"This was Garstang's job. I regularly checked his decisions on the display board. Occasionally he found it necessary to consult; not often."

"When you use the radio, what is your routine? What do you say?"

"It is very simple. I say: 'The Anome instructs that such an act be accomplished.' That is the end of it."

"Very good. Call now the Office of Proclamations, and all the rest. This is what you must say:

'In response to the depredations of the Roguskhoi I proclaim a state of emergency. Shant must now mobilize its strength against these creatures and destroy them.' "

15

Sajarano shook his head. "I cannot say that; you must do so yourself." He seemed disoriented. His hands twitched; his eyes jerked from side to side, his skin showed an ugly yellowish tint.

"Why can't you say it?" asked Etzwane.

"It is contrary to my inner soul. I cannot participate in your venture. It means chaos!"

"If we don't destroy the Roguskhoi it means no more Shant, which is worse," Etzwane said. "Show me how to use the radio."

Sajarano's mouth trembled; for a moment Etzwane thought that he would refuse. Then he said, "Push that switch. Turn the green knob until the green light glows. Push the button of the agency you choose to call. Press the purple button to signal the monitor. When the purple light flashes, speak."

Etzwane approached the bench; Sajarano drew back a few steps. Etzwane pretended to study the equipment. Sajarano darted for the door, passed through, swung it shut. Etzwane hurled himself into the opening; the two struggled. Etzwane was young and strong; Sajarano thrust with hysterical frenzy. Their two heads, on opposite sides of the opening, were only inches apart. Sajarano's eyes bulged, his mouth hung open. His feet slipped, the door swung back.

Etzwane said politely, "Who lives here beside yourself?"

"Only my staff," muttered Sajarano.

"The radio can wait," said Etzwane. "First I must deal with you."

Sajarano stood with sagging shoulders. Etzwane said, "Come. Leave these doors open. I want you to instruct your staff that I and my friends will be taking up residence here."

Sajarano gave a fatalistic sigh. "What are your plans for me?"

"If you cooperate, your life is your own."

"I will do my best," said Sajarano, in the voice of an old man. "I must try, I must try. . . . I will call Aganthe, my major-domo. How many persons will be coming? I live a solitary life."

"I'll have to take counsel with them."

CHAPTER TWO

Sajarano lay drugged in his bedchamber; Etzwane stood in the hall. What to do with the corpse? He did not know. Unwise to order the servants to remove it. Let it stay then, until he had organized matters. . . . Lovely Jurjin! What a waste of beauty and vitality! He could summon no more fury against Sajarano; such emotion seemed stale. Sajarano clearly was insane.

Now: the proclamation. Etzwane returned to the radio room, where he wrote what he considered a succinct and emphatic message. Then he manipulated the array of dials and buttons as Sajarano had instructed. He first signalled the Office of Proclamations.

The purple light flashed.

Etzwane spoke. "The Anome orders dissemination throughout Shant of the following proclamation:

"In response to the dangerous presence of the Roguskhoi in our midst, the Anome proclaims a state of emergency, effective immediately.

"For several years the Anome has attempted to deal with the invaders on the basis of peaceful persuasion. These efforts have failed; we now must act with the total force of our nation; the Roguskhoi will be exterminated or repelled into Palasedra.

"The Roguskhoi exhibit an unnatural lust, from which many women have suffered. To minimize further episodes of this type, the Anome orders that all women depart those cantons adjacent to the Wildlands. They are to travel to maritime cantons, where the authorities must prepare safe and comfortable accommodations.

"Simultaneously, the authorities in each canton shall organize a militia of able men, to the number of at least one man for each one hundred persons of population. Further orders in this regard will be forthcoming. Cantonal authorities, however, must immediately start the process of recruitment. Delay will not be tolerated.

"The Anome will make additional proclamations at an appropriate time. My Executive Aide is Gastel Etzwane. He will coordinate the separate efforts and speak with my voice. He must be obeyed in all regards."

Etzwane called the Chief Discriminator of Garwiy and once again read his proclamation. "Gastel Etzwane must be obeyed as if he were the Anome himself. Is this clear?"

The Chief Discriminators voice returned: "Gastel Etzwane will be accorded full cooperation. I may say, your Excellency, that this policy will be welcomed throughout Shant. We are pleased that you are taking action!"

"It is not I, declared Etzwane. "The folk of Shant are taking action. I only direct their efforts. I alone can do nothing!"

"This of course is correct," came the response. "Are there further instructions?"

"Yes. I want the most able technists of Garwiy assembled tomorrow at noon in the Corporation Offices, in order that I may take advice upon weapons and weapons production."

19

"I will see to this."

"For the moment, that is all."

Etzwane explored Sershan Palace. The staff watched him askance, muttering and wondering. Never had Etzwane imagined such elegance. He found richness accumulated over thousands of years: glass columns inlaid with silver symbols; rooms of pale blue opening upon rooms of old rose; whole walls worked into vitran* landscapes; furniture and porcelain of the far past; magnificent rugs of Maseach and Cansume; a display of distorted gold masks, stolen at fearful risk from the interior of Caraz.

Such a palace, mused Etzwane, could be his own if he desired. Absurd that Gastel Etzwane, casually fathered by the druithine Dystar upon Eathre of Rhododendron Way, should be – why not admit the situation? – effectively Anome of Shant!

Etzwane gave a melancholy shrug. During his youth he had known penury; each florin he could save represented the fifteen-hundredth part of his mothers freedom. Now the wealth of Shant lay open to his hand! It held no appeal. . . . And what to do about the corpse in the morning room?

In the library he sat down to ponder. . . . Sajarano

Vitran: a process of visual representation unique to Garwiy. The artist and his apprentice use minute rods of coloured glass a quarter of an inch long, one twentieth of an inch in diameter. The rods are cemented lengthwise against a back-plate of frosted glass. The finished work, illuminated from behind, becomes a landscape, portrait, or pattern, vital beyond all other representational processes, combining radiance, chromatic range, flexibility, refinement, detail, and scope. Inordinate effort and time is required to produce even a small work, with approximately sixty thousand individual rods comprising each square foot of finished surface.

seemed not a villain, but a figure of doom. Why could he not have expressed himself frankly? Why could they not have worked together? Etzwane reviewed the dismal circumstances. Sajarano could not be kept drugged indefinitely; on the other hand he could not be trusted in any other condition – except dead.

Etzwane grimaced. He longed for the presence of Ifness, who seemed never to lack resource. In the absence of Ifness, allies of any sort would be welcome.

There was always Frolitz and his troupe: the Pink-Black-Azure-Deep Greeners. A ridiculous idea, which Etzwane rejected at once . . . who else? Two names entered his mind: Dystar, his father, and Jerd Finnerack.

Essentially he knew little of either. Dystar was not even aware of his existence. Etzwane nevertheless had heard Dystar's music, and had been provided evidence as to Dystar's inner self. As for Finnerack, Etzwane remembered only a sturdy youth with a determined brown face and sun-bleached blond hair. Finnerack had been kind to the desperate waif Gastel Etzwane; he had encouraged Etzwane to attempt escape from Angwin Junction, an island in the air. What had become of Jerd Finnerack?

Etzwane returned to the radio room. He called the Chief Discriminators office and requested that information regarding Jerd Finnerack be solicited from the balloon-way office.

Etzwane looked in upon Sajarano, who lay supine in drugged slumber. Etzwane scowled and left the room. He summoned a footman to the great parlour and sent him to Fontenays Inn, where he was to find Frolitz and fetch him to Sershan Palace.

In due course Frolitz arrived, at once truculent and apprehensive. At the sight of Etzwane he stopped short, jerked his head back in suspicion.

"Come in, come in," said Etzwane. Waving away the footman, he led Frolitz into the great parlour. "Sit down. Will you take tea?"

"Certainly," said Frolitz. "Are you about to divulge the reason for your presence here?"

"It is a queer set of circumstances," said Etzwane. "As you know I recently submitted a five hundred florin petition to the Anome."

"Of this I am aware; more fool you."

"Not altogether. The Anome had come to share my views; he therefore asked me to assist in what will be a great campaign against the Roguskhoi."

Frolitz gaped in astonishment. "You? Gastel Etzwane the musician? What fantasy is this?"

"No fantasy. Someone must do these jobs. I agreed; additionally, I volunteered your services in this same cause."

Frolitz' grizzled jaw dropped even further. Then his eyes took on a sardonic gleam. "Of course! Precisely what is needed to send the Roguskhoi scuttling: old Frolitz and his savage troupe! I should have thought of it myself."

"The situation is extraordinary," said Etzwane. "Still you need only accept the evidence of your senses."

Frolitz gave a qualified assent. "We seem to be sitting like Aesthetes in an uncommonly luxurious palace. What next?"

"It is as I told you originally. We are to assist the Anome."

Frolitz examined Etzwane's face with renewed suspicion. "One matter must be clear beyond any reconsideration: I am not a warrior; I am too old to fight."

"Neither you nor I will actually wield a sword," said Etzwane. "Our duties are to be somewhat clandestine and – naturally – profitable."

"In what regard and to what degree?"

"This is Sershan Palace," said Etzwane. "We are to take up residence here: you, I, the entire troupe. We will be fed and lodged like Aesthetes. Our duties are simple, but before I tell you more I want to learn your opinion of this appointment."

Frolitz scratched his head, working his sparse grey hair into a bristle. "You spoke of profit. This sounds like the Gastel Etzwane of old, who nurtured each florin as if it were a dying saint. All else carries the flavour of hallucination."

"We sit here in Sershan Palace. Hallucination? I think not. The proposal is unexpected, but, as you know, strange things happen."

"True! The musician lives a startling life. . . . I certainly have no objection to occupying Sershan Palace, for as long as the Sershans permit. This would not be your idea of a prank, to see old Frolitz hauled off to Stonebreakers' Island, protesting innocence all the while?"

"Absolutely not, I swear it. What of the troupe?"

"Would they ignore such an opportunity? What then would be our duties – assuming the matter not to be a hoax?"

"It is a peculiar situation," said Etzwane. "The Anome wants Sajarano of Sershan kept under observation. To be blunt, Sajarano is to be held under house-arrest. That is to be our function."

Frolitz grunted. "Now I am beset by another fear: if the Anome starts to employ his musicians as jailers, he may decide to use the displaced jailers as musicians."

"The process will not go so far," said Etzwane. "Essentially, I was instructed to recruit a few trustworthy persons; I thought first of the troupe. As I say, we will all be well paid; in fact, I can requisition new instruments for everyone in the troupe: the best woodhorns, blackbirk khitans with bronze hinges, silver tipples, whatever may be needed or desired, and no thought for expense."

Frolitz' jaw dropped again. "You can do all this?"

"I can."

"If so, you may count upon the cooperation of the troupe. Indeed, we long have needed such a period of relaxation."

Sajarano occupied chambers high in a tower of pearlglass to the back of the palace. Etzwane found him primly at ease on a green satin couch, toying with a beautiful set of puzzle ivories. His face was drawn; his skin showed the colour and texture of old paper. His greeting was reserved; he refused to meet Etzwane's gaze.

"We have acted," said Etzwane. "The force of Shant is now committed against the Roguskhoi."

"I hope that you find the problems as easy to resolve as to create," said Sajarano curtly.

Etzwane seated himself across from Sajarano on a white wood chair. "You have not altered your views?"

"When they derive from earnest study over a period of years? Of course not."

"I hope, however, that you agree to desist from adverse actions?"

"The power is yours," said Sajarano. "I must now obey."

"So you said before," noted Etzwane. "Then you attempted to poison me."

24

Sajarano gave a disinterested shrug. "I could only do as my inner voice dictated."

"Hmmf. . . . What does it dictate now?"

"Nothing. I have known tragedy and my only wish is for seclusion."

"This you shall have," said Etzwane. "For a brief period, until events order themselves, a company of musicians with whom I am associated will ensure this seclusion. It is the minimal inconvenience I can impose on you. I hope you will take it in good part."

"So long as they do not rehearse or indulge in destructive horseplay."

Etzwane looked out the window towards the forests of the Ushkadel. "How should we remove the corpse from the morning room?"

Sajarano said in a low voice: "Push the button yonder; it will summon Aganthe."

The major-domo appeared. "In the morning room you will find a corpse," said Sajarano. "Bury it, sink it in the Sualle, dispose of it as you like, but with all discretion. Then clean the morning room."

Aganthe bowed and departed.

Sajarano turned to Etzwane. "What else do you require?"

"I will need to disburse public money. What procedure do I follow in this regard?"

Sajarano's lips twitched with bitter amusement. He put aside the ivories. "Come."

They descended to Sajarano's private study, where for a moment Sajarano stood in cogitation. Etzwane wondered if he planned another grim surprise, and ostentatiously put his hand into his pouch. Sajarano gave the slightest of shrugs, as if dismissing from his mind whatever idea had entered. From a cabinet he extracted a packet of vouchers. Etzwane cautiously came forward, finger on the yellow button. But Sajarano's defiance had waned. He muttered, "Your policies are far too bold for me. Perhaps they are right; perhaps I have buried my head in the sand. . . . Sometimes I feel as if I have been living a dream."

In a dull voice he instructed Etzwane in the use of the vouchers.

"Let us have no misunderstandings," Etzwane told Sajarano. "You must not leave the palace, use the radio, send the servants on missions, or entertain friends. We intend you no inconvenience so long as you do nothing to provoke our suspicion."

Etzwane then summoned Frolitz and made him known to Sajarano. Frolitz spoke with a waggish cordiality. "This for me is unfamiliar employment I trust that our association will be placid."

"It will be so on my part," said Sajarano in a bitter voice. "Well then what else do you require?"

"At the moment nothing."

Sajarano went off to his chambers in the pearl-glass tower Frolitz said in a quizzical voice, "Your duties appear to exceed the simple jailing of Sajarano."

"Quite true," said Etzwane. "If you are curious –"

"Tell me nothing!" cried Frolitz. "The less my knowledge the greater my innocence!"

"As you wish." Etzwane showed Frolitz the stairs leading to the radio room. "Remember! Sajarano must definitely be barred from this area!"

"A bold restriction," said Frolitz, "in view of the fact that he owns the palace."

"Regardless, it must be applied. Someone must remain on guard here at all times, day and night."

"Inconvenient when we wish to rehearse," grumbled Frolitz.

"Rehearse here in front of the stairs." He pushed the call-button; Aganthe appeared.

"We will be disrupting your routines for a certain period," said Etzwane. "To be candid, the Anome has ordained a mild form of house-arrest for Sajarano. Master Frolitz and his associates will be in charge of arrangements. They are anxious to obtain your complete cooperation."

Aganthe bowed. "My responsibility is to his Excellency Sajarano; he has instructed me to obey your orders; this I will do."

"Very good. I now instruct you not to listen to any orders Sajarano may utter in conflict with our official duties. Is that clear?"

"Yes, your Excellency."

"If Sajarano gives such an order, you must consult me or Master Frolitz. I cannot emphasize this too strongly. In the morning room you have seen the consequence of incorrect conduct."

"I understand completely, your Excellency." Aganthe departed.

Etzwane told Frolitz: "From now on you must control events. Be suspicious! Sajarano is a resourceful man."

"Do you consider me any the less so?" demanded Frolitz. "Remember when we last played *Kheriteri Melanchine?* Who instantly transposed to the seventh tone when Lurnous embarrassed us all? Is not this resource? Who locked Barndart the balladist in the privy when he persisted in song? What then of resource?"

"I have no fears," Etzwane replied.

Frolitz went off to inform the troupe in regard to their new duties; Etzwane returned to Sajarano's study and there drew up a voucher against public funds to the sum of twenty-thousand florins – enough, he calculated, to cover ordinary and extraordinary expenses for the near future.

At the Bank of Shant the sum of twenty thousand florins was paid over without question or formality; never in his life had Etzwane thought to control so much money!

The function of money was its use; at a nearby haberdashery Etzwane selected garments he deemed consonant with his new role: a rich jacket of purple and green velour, dark green trousers, a black velvet cape with a pale green lining, the finest boots to be had. . . . He surveyed himself in the haberdasher's massive carbon-fume mirror, matching this splendid young patrician with the Gastel Etzwane of earlier days, who never spent a florin on other than urgent need.

The Aesthetic Corporation was housed in the Jurisdictionary, a vast construction of purple, green, and blue glass at the back of the Corporation Plaza. The first two levels dated from the Middle Pandamons; the next four levels the six towers and eleven domes, had been completed ten years before the Fourth Palasedran War, and by a miracle had escaped the great bombardment.

Etzwane went to the office of Aun Sharah, Chief Discriminator of Garwiy, on the second level of the Jurisdictionary. "Be so good as to announce me," he told the clerk. "I am Gastel Etzwane".

Aun Sharah himself came forth: a handsome man

with thick silver hair worn close to his head, a fine aquiline nose, a wide, half-smiling mouth. He wore the simplest of dark grey tunics, ornamented only by a pair of small silverwood shoulder-clips: a costume so distinguished that Etzwane wondered if his own garments might not seem over-sumptuous by comparison.

The Chief Discriminator inspected Etzwane with easy curiosity. "Come into my rooms, if you will."

They went to a large, high-ceilinged office overlooking the Corporation Plaza. Like Aun Sharah's garments, the furnishings of his office were simple and elegant. Aun Sharah indicated a chair for Etzwane and settled upon a couch at the side of the room. Etzwane envied him his ease; Aun Sharah was distracted by no trace of self-consciousness. All his attention, so it appeared, was fixed upon Etzwane, who enjoyed no such advantage.

"You know of the new state of affairs," said Etzwane. "The Anome has committed the power of Shant against the Roguskhoi."

"Somewhat belatedly" murmured Aun Sharah.

Etzwane thought the remark a trifle insouciant. "Be that as it may, we must now arm ourselves. In this regard, the Anome has appointed me his Executive Aide; I speak with his voice."

Aun Sharah leaned back into the couch. "Isn't it strange? Only a day or so ago a certain Gastel Etzwane was the object of an official search. I assume you to be the same person."

Etzwane regarded the Chief Discriminator with pointed coolness. "The Anome sought me; he found me. I put certain facts at his disposal; he reacted as you know."

"Wisely! Or such is my opinion," said Aun Sharah. "What, may I ask, were the 'facts'?"

"The mathematical certainty of disaster unless we gave instant battle. Have you arranged the assembly of technists?"

"The arrangements are being made. How many persons did you wish to consult?"

Etzwane glanced sharply at the Chief Discriminator, who seemed bland and relaxed. Etzwane feigned perplexity. "Did not the Anome issue a specific command?"

"I believe that he left the number indefinite."

"In that case, assemble the most expert and well-regarded authorities, from whom we can select a chairman or director of research. I want you to be on hand as well. Our first objective is to create a corps of capable men to implement the Anome's policies."

Aun Sharah nodded slowly and thoughtfully. "How much progress has been made along these lines?"

Etzwane began to find the casual gaze somewhat too knowing. He said, "Not a great deal. Names are still under discussion. . . . In regard to the person Jerd Finnerack, what have you learned?"

Aun Sharah picked up a slip of paper. He read: " 'Jerd Finnerack: an indentured employee of the balloon-way. Born in the village Ispero in the eastern region of Morningshore. His father, a berry grower, used the child's person as security against a loan; when he failed his obligation the child was seized. Finnerack has proved a recalcitrant worker. On one occasion he criminally loosed a balloon from the switching wheel at Angwin Junction, resulting in extensive charges against the company. These costs were added to his indenture. He works now at Camp Three in Canton Glaiy, which is an accommodation for refractory workers. His indenture totals somewhat over two thousand florins.' " He handed the paper to Etzwane.

"Why, may I ask, are you interested in Jerd Finnerack?"

More stiffly than ever Etzwane said, "I understand your natural interest; the Anome, however, insists upon total discretion. In regard to another matter: he Anome has ordered a movement of women to the maritime cantons. Unpleasant incidents must be minimized. In each canton at least six monitors should be appointed to hear complaints and note down particulars for subsequent action. I want you to appoint competent officers and station them as quickly as possible."

"The measure is essential," Aun Sharah agreed. "I will dispatch men from my own staff to organize the groups."

"I leave the matter in your hands."

Etzwane departed the Office of the Chief Discriminator. On the whole, matters had gone well. Aun Sharah's calm visage undoubtedly concealed a seethe of clever formulations, which might or might not persuade him to mischief. More than ever Etzwane felt the need of a completely trustworthy and trusted ally. Alone, his position was precarious indeed.

He returned by a roundabout route to Sershan Palace. For a period he thought that someone followed him, but when he stepped through Pomegranate Portal and waited in the crimson gloom behind the pillar, no one came past, and when he continued, the way behind seemed clear.

CHAPTER THREE

Exactly at noon Etzwane entered the main conference hall of the Jurisdictionary. Looking neither right nor left he marched to the speaker's platform; placing his hands on the solid silver rail, he looked out over the attentive faces.

"Gentlemen: the Anome has prepared a message, which by his instructions I will read to you." Etzwane brought forth a sheet of parchment. "Here are the words of the Anome:

'Greetings to the technical aristocracy of Garwiy! Today I solicit your counsel in regard to the Roguskhoi. I have long hoped to repel these creatures without violence, but my efforts have been in vain; now we must fight.

'I have ordered formation of an army, but this is only half the work; effective weapons are needed.

'Here is the exact problem. The Roguskhoi warrior is massive, savage, fearless. His principal weapons are a metal cudgel and a scimitar: this latter both a cutting and a throwing weapon, effective to a distance of fifty yards or more. In hand-to-hand combat an ordinary man is helpless. Our soldiers therefore must be armed with weapons useful to a range of one hundred yards, or preferably more.

'I place this problem in your hands and direct that you immediately concentrate your efforts upon this single task. All the resources of Shant will be at your disposal.

'Naturally it is necessary that the effort be organized. So now I wish you to choose from among your present number a chairman to supervise your efforts.

'For my Executive Aide I have appointed the person who reads this message, Gastel Etzwane. He speaks with my voice; you will make your reports to him and follow his recommendations.

'I reiterate the urgency of this matter. Our militia is gathering and soon will need weapons.' "

Etzwane put down the paper and looked out over the ranked faces. "Are there any questions?"

A stout and somewhat florid man rose ponderously to his feet. "The requirements are less than clear. What sort of weapons does the Anome have in mind?"

"Weapons to kill the Roguskhoi, and to drive them back, at minimal risk to the user," said Etzwane.

"This is all very well," complained the stout man, "but we are afforded no illumination. The Anome should provide a general set of specifications, or at least basic designs! Are we required to grope in the dark?"

"The Anome is no technist," said Etzwane. "You people are the technists! Develop your own specifications and designs! If energy weapons can be produced, so much the better. If not, contrive whatever is practical and feasible. All over Shant the armies are forming; they need the tools of war. The Anome cannot ordain weapons out of thin air; they must be designed and produced by you, the technists!"

The florid man looked uncertainly from right to left, then sat down. In the back row Etzwane noticed Aun Sharah, with a musing ruminative smile on his face.

A tall man with black eyes burning from a waxen face rose to his feet. "Your remarks are to the point, and we will do our best. But remember: we are technists, not innovators. We refine processes rather than create concepts."

"If you can't do the work, find someone who can," said Etzwane. "I delegate to you the responsibility for this task. Create or die."

Another man spoke: "A matter to affect our thinking is the size of the proposed army. This controls the number of weapons required. Elegance might well be less important than availability and effectiveness."

"Correct," said Etzwane. "The army will number between twenty thousand and one hundred thousand, depending upon the difficulty of the campaign. I might add that weapons are only the most urgent need. We want communication equipment so that the commanders of various groups may coordinate their efforts. Your chairman should appoint a team to develop such equipment."

Etzwane stood waiting for further inquiries, but a glum and dubious silence persisted. Etzwane said, "I will leave you to your work. Select a chairman, a man whom you know to be competent, decisive, and, if necessary harsh. He will designate work groups as he deems practical. Questions or recommendations will reach me through the Chief Discriminator, Aun Sharah."

Without further words Etzwane bowed and departed the way he had come.

In the pavilion before the Jurisdictionary Aun Sharah

approached Etzwane. "The processes go into motion," he said. "I hope efficiently. These folk have no experience in creative work, and if I may say so, the Faceless Man seems in this case indecisive."

"How so?" asked Etzwane in a neutral voice.

"Ordinarily he would request dossiers and evaluations of each man; he would then appoint a chairman and give precise orders. The technists are now puzzled and uncertain; they lack a sure initiative."

Etzwane gave a disinterested shrug. "The Anome has many calculations to make. It is essential that other men share the load."

"Of course, if they are capable, and given a programme."

"They must develop their own programme."

"It is an interesting idea," admitted Aun Sharah. "I hope that it will work."

"It must work, if we are to survive. The Anome cannot fight the Roguskhoi with his own hands. I presume that you have examined my background?"

Aun Sharah assented without embarrassment. "You are, or were, a musician with the well-considered troupe of Master Frolitz."

"I am a musician. I know other musicians in a way you could not know them, if you prepared a hundred dossiers."

Aun Sharah rubbed his chin. "So then?"

"Suppose the Anome wished to organize a troupe of Shant's best musicians. No doubt you would compile dossiers and he would make a selection: would these musicians play well; would they complement each other? I suspect otherwise. My point is this: no outsider can effectively organize a group of experts; they must organize themselves. Such is the Anome's present conviction."

"I will be interested in the progress made by the group," said Aun Sharah. "What weapons do you expect from them?"

Etzwane turned Aun Sharah a cold side-glance. "What do I know of weapons? I have no expectations, any more than the Anome."

"Natural enough. Well then, I must return to my office to reorganize my staff." Aun Sharah went his way.

Etzwane crossed the plaza and stepped down into the Rosewalk. At a secluded table he sipped a cup of tea and considered his progress to date. It was, he thought, significant; important forces had been set into motion. Women were moving to relative safety in the maritime cantons; at best there would be no more breeding of new Roguskhoi, at worst the Roguskhoi would raid further afield. The militia had been ordained; the technists had been instructed to produce weapons. Sajarano was guarded by Frolitz; Aun Sharah, an uncertain quantity, must be dealt with gingerly.

For the moment he had done all in his power.... Someone had left a copy of *Aernid Koromatik** on a nearby chair; Etzwane picked it up and scanned the coloured patterns. Pale blue and green characters informed of social events and trivial gossip, with pink and old rose titillations; these columns Etzwane ignored. He read the lavender proclamation of the Anome. In various shades of indigo and green† opinions of well-known persons

*Literally "Chromatic Envelope," to signify an inclusive range of every kind of news.

†The exact quality of blue or green measured the quoted person's prestige: Reputation, vanity, ridicule, popularity, pomposity: all were implicit in the depths, variations, and overtones of the colours employed – a symbology of great subtlety.

were set forth: all evinced approval. "At last the Anome turns his vast power against the savage hordes," declared the Aesthete Santangelo of Ferathilen, in ultramarine symbols. "The folk of Shant can now relax."

Etzwane's lip curled; he gave the journal a shake. At the bottom of the page a border of brown enclosed an ochre-yellow message: news of morbid and dreadful nature. The Roguskhoi had moved in a strength estimated at over five hundred into the Farwan Valley of Canton Lor-Asphen, killing many men and enslaving a large number of women. "They have established a camp; they show no signs of retreating into the Hwan. Do they then regard the valley as conquered territory?

"The women of Lor-Asphen are now being evacuated into Cantons Morningshore and Esterland as rapidly as possible. Unfortunately, the Anome has not yet mustered sufficient strength to deal a counterblow. It is hoped that there will be no more such terrible acts."

Etzwane laid the paper aside, then on second thought folded it into the pocket of his cape. For a space he sat watching the folk at nearby tables. They chatted; they were charming; their sensibilities were subtle. . . . Into the garden now came the florid technist, he who had arisen first to ask questions. He wore a pale green cloak over his black and white; he joined a group of his friends at a table near where Etzwane sat: two men and two women, wearing rich robes of blue, green, purple, and white. They leaned forward as the stout man spoke in an animated voice. Etzwane listened: "– insane, insane! This is not our function; what do we know of such things? The Anome expects miracles; he wants bricks without furnishing straw! Let him provide the weapons; is he not the power of Shant?"

One of his companions spoke a few words, to which the florid technist made an impatient retort: "It is all nonsense! I intend to draw up a petition of protest; the Anome will surely see reason."

Etzwane listened in a rigidity of disbelief that dissolved into fury. Only minutes before he had enjoined selfless exertion upon this fat, stupid man. Already he spread defeatism! Etzwane brought out the pulse-emitter; he punched the studs to the man's code. . . . He stopped short of touching yellow; instead he went to glare down into the man's suddenly blank face. "I heard your remarks," said Etzwane. "Do you know how close you came to losing your head? One eighth of an inch, the press of a button."

"I spoke idly, no more," cried the man in a plaintive rush of words. "Must you take everything at face value?"

"How else? It is how I intend my words. Say goodbye to your friends; you have suddenly become a member of the Garwiy militia. I hope you fight as well as you talk."

"The militia! Impossible! My work –"

" 'Impossible'?" Etzwane ostentatiously made a note of the man's colour code. "I will explain circumstances to the Anome; you had best set your affairs in order."

Stunned, white-faced, the man slumped back in his chair.

Etzwane rode a diligence to Sershan Palace. He found Sajarano in the rooftop garden, playing with a prismatic toy. Etzwane stood watching a moment. Sajarano moved coloured spots of light along a white bar, small mouth pursed, eyes studiously averted from Etzwane.

Under that poet's forehead what occurred? What impulses actuated those small hands, once so quick and powerful? Etzwane, already in a grim mood, found the bafflement intolerable. He brought forth the newspaper and placed it in front of Sajarano, who put aside the toy to read. He glanced up at Etzwane. "Events rush together. History occurs."

Etzwane pointed to the brown and yellow. "What do you make of this?"

"Tragedy."

"You agree that the Roguskhoi are our enemies?"

"It cannot be denied."

"How would you deal with them, had you power once again?"

Sajarano started to speak, then looked down at his toy. "The avenues of action all lead into dark mist."

Sajarano might well be the victim of mental affliction, thought Etzwane; in fact, this almost certainly was the case. He asked, "How did you become Anome?"

"My father was Anome before me. When he grew old he passed on the power." Looking off into the sky, Sajarano smiled in sad recollection. "The transfer was in this case simple; it is not always so."

"Who was to have been Anome after you?"

Sajarano's smile faded; he frowned in concentration. "At one time I inclined towards Arnold of Cham, whom I considered qualified by birth, intellect, and integrity. I reconsidered. The Anome must be clever and harsh; he can afford no qualms." Sajarano's fingers gave a convulsive twitch. "The terrible deeds I have done! In Haviosq to alarm the sacred birds is a crime. In Fordume the apprentice jade carver must die if his masterwork cracks. Arnold of Cham, a reasonable man, could not enforce laws so grotesque. I considered a man more flexible: Aun

39

Sharah, the Chief Discriminator. He is cool, clever, capable of detachment.... I rejected Aun Sharah for reason of style, and settled upon Garstang, now dead.... The whole subject is irrelevant."

Etzwane pondered a moment. "Did Aun Sharah know that he was under consideration?"

Sajarano shrugged and picked up the toy. "He is a perceptive man. It is hard to conceal the exercise of power from a person in his position."

Etzwane went to the radio room. He adjusted the filter to disassociate himself from the previous message; he then called Aun Sharah. "This is Gastel Etzwane. I have taken counsel with the Anome. He has ordered that you and I go forth as plenipotentiaries to all regions of Shant. You are required to visit the cantons east of the Jardeen and north of the Wildlands, including Shkoriy, Lor-Asphen Haghead, and Morningshore. I am assigned the cantons to west and south. We are to stimulate and, if necessary coerce the mobilization and training of the various militias. Do you have any questions?"

There was a brief silence. "You used the word 'coerce'. How is this to be effected?"

"We are to note particulars of recalcitrance; the Anome will inflict penalties. Conditions vary. I can offer no explicit instructions; you must use your best judgment."

Aun Shara's voice was a trifle bleak: "When am I to leave?"

"Tomorrow. Your first cantons should perhaps be Wale Purple Fan, Anglesiy, Jardeen, and Conduce; then you can take the balloon-way at Brassei Junction for the far west. I go first to Wild Rose, Maiy, Erevan, and Shade, then take balloon for Esterland. For funds we are to issue drafts against the Bank of Shant, and naturally stint ourselves nothing."

"Very well," said Aun Sharah without enthusiasm. "We must do what is required."

CHAPTER FOUR

The balloon *Iridixn*, requisitioned by Etzwane, swayed at the loading platform: a triple-segmented slab of withe, cord, and glossy film. The winch-tender was Casallo, a young man of airs and graces, who performed the sensitive acts of his trade with bored disdain. Etzwane stepped into the gondola; Casallo, already in his compartment, asked: "What, sir, are your orders?"

"I want to visit Jamilo, Vervei, Sacred Hill in Erevan, Lanteen in Shade. Then we will proceed directly across Shant to Esterland."

"As you wish, sir." Casallo barely stifled a yawn. Over his ear he wore a sprig of purple arasma, souvenir of last night's revelry. Etzwane watched with suspicion as Casallo checked the action of his winches, tested gas valves and ballast release, then dropped the semaphore. "Up we go."

The station gang walked the judas dolly down the slot, allowing the balloon a medium scope. Casallo negligently adjusted cant and aspect to lay the balloon on a broad reach across the wind. The guys were detached from the sheave on the judas dolly, the running dolly was released from its clamp; the balloon slid away; the dolly whirred cheerfully down the slot. Casallo adjusted the guys with the air of a man inventing a new process; the balloon perceptibly accelerated and sailed east through Jardeen Gap. The Ushkadel became a dark blur to the rear, and presently they entered Wild Rose, where among wooded hillocks, vales, ponds, and placid meadows the Aesthetes of Garwiy maintained their country estates.

Approaching the market town Jamilo, the balloon showed its orange semaphore and luffed; the station gang trapped the running dolly and diverted it onto a siding, where they clamped it to the slot. They caught the guys in the sheaves of the judas dolly and, hauling the judas dolly up the slot towards the depot, drew the balloon to the ground.

Etzwane went to the canton Moot-hall, which he found quiet and unoccupied. The Anome's proclamation had been posted, but no person of authority had come past to see it.

In a fury Etzwane went to the clerk's cubicle, where he demanded an explanation. The clerk hobbled forth and blinked without comprehension as Etzwane criticized his conduct. "Why did you not summon the councilman?" stormed Etzwane. "Are you so ignorant that you cannot understand the urgency of the message? You are discharged! clear out of this office and be grateful if the Anome does not take your head!"

"During all my tenure events have moved with deliberation," quavered the clerk. "How was I to know that this particular business must go at the speed of lightning?"

"Now you know! How do you summon the councilmen to an emergency session?"

"I don't know; we have never experienced an emergency."

"Does Jamilo boast a brigade for the control of fires?"

43

"Yes indeed. The gong is yonder."

"Go sound the gong!"

The folk of Maiy were commerciants: a tall, dark-haired, dark-skinned people, suave and quiet of demeanour. They lived in octagonal houses with tall, eight-sided roofs; from the centre of which projected chimneys, each taller than the one before; and indeed the height of a man's chimney measured his prestige. The canton's administrative centre, Vervei, was not so much a town as an agglomeration of small industries, producing toys, wooden bowls, trays, candelabra, doors, furniture. Etzwane found the industries working at full speed and the First Negociant of Maiy admitted that he had taken no steps to implement the Anome's proclamaion. "It is very difficult for us to move quickly," he stated with a disarming smile. "We have contracts which limit our freedom; you must realize that this is our busy season. Surely the Anome in his power and wisdom can control the Roguskhoi without turning our lives upside down!"

Etzwane ostentatiously noted the code of the Negociant's torc. "If a single one of your concerns opens for business before an able militia is formed and at drill, you will lose your head. The war against the Roguskhoi supersedes all else! Is so much clear?"

The Negociant's thin face became grave. "It is difficult to understand how –"

Etzwane said: "You have exactly ten seconds to start obeying the Anome's orders. Can you understand this?"

The Negociant touched his torc. "I understand completely."

In Conduce Etzwane found confusion. Looming above

the horizon to the southeast stood the first peaks of the Hwan; an arm of Shellflower Bay extended almost as close from the north. "Should we send our women north? Or should we prepare to receive women from the mountains? The Fowls say one thing, the Fruits* another. The Fowls want to form a militia of young men, because old men are better with the flocks; the Fruits want to draft old men, because young men are needed to harvest the fruit. Only the Anome can solve our problems!"

"Use young Fowls and old Fruits," Etzwane told him, "but act with decision! If the Anome learned of your delay he'd take heads from Fowls and Fruits alike."

In Shade, under the very loom of the Hwan, the Roguskhoi were a known danger. On many occasions small bands had been glimpsed in the upper valleys, where now no man dared to go; three small settlements had been raided. Etzwane found no need to stress the need for action. A large number of women had been sent north; groups of the new militia were already in the process of organization.

In the company of the First Duke of Shade Etzwane watched two squads drilling with staves and poles, to simulate swords and spears, at opposite ends of the Lanteen Arena. The squads showed noticeable differences in costume, zeal, and general competence. The first wore well-cut garments of indigo and mulberry, with green leather boots; they sprang back and forth; they lunged, feinted, swaggered; they called jocular comments back and forth as they exercised. The second group, in work clothes and sandals, drilled without fervour and spoke only in surly mutters. Etzwane inquired as to the disparity.

*Fowls and Fruits: the rival factions of Conduce, representing the poultry industry and the fruit growers.

"Our policy has not yet been made firm," said the First Duke. "Some of those summoned to duty sent indentured bondsmen, who show no great zest. I am not sure if the system will prove feasible; perhaps persons who find themselves unable to drill should send two bondsmen, rather than one. Perhaps the practice should be totally discouraged. There are arguments for all points of view."

Etzwane said, "The defence of Shant is a privilege accorded only to free men. By joining the militia the indentured man automatically dissolves his debts. Be so good as to announce this fact to the group yonder; then let us judge their zeal."

The balloon-way led into the Wildlands, the *Iridixn* now sailing at the full length of its guys, the better to catch the most direct draughts of wind. At Angwin an endless cable drew the *Iridixn* across Angwin Gorge to Angwin Junction, an island in the sky, from which Etzwane had escaped long ago with the unwitting assistance of Jerd Finnerack.

The *Iridixn* continued southeast, across the most dramatic regions of the Wildlands. Casallo scrutinized the panorama through binoculars. He pointed down into a mountain valley. "You're concerned with the Roguskhoi? Look there! A whole tribe before your eyes!"

Taking the binoculars Etzwane observed a large number of quiet dark spots, perhaps as many as four hundred, beside a stockade of thorn bush. From under a dozen great cauldrons came wisps of smoke, to drift away down the valley. Etzwane examined the interior of the stockade. Certain ambiguous bunches of rags he saw to be huddles of women, to the number of possibly a hundred. At the back of the stockade, under the shelter of a rude shed, were perhaps others.... Etzwane examined other areas of the camp. Each Roguskhoi squatted alone and self-sufficient; a few mended harness, rubbed grease on their bodies, fed wood into the fires under the cauldrons. None, so far as Etzwane could detect, so much as glanced up at the passing balloon or towards the dolly which rolled whirring through the slot not a quarter-mile distant.... The *Iridixn* passed around a crag of rock; the valley could no longer be seen.

Etzwane put the binoculars on the rack. "Where do they get their swords? Those cauldrons are metal – a fortune wouldn't buy them."

Casallo laughed. "Metal cauldrons and they cook grass, leaves, black worms, dead ahulph, and live ones too, anything they can get down their throats. I've watched them through the binoculars."

"Do they ever show any interest in the balloon? They could cause trouble if they meddled with the slot."

"They've never bothered the slot," said Casallo. "Many things they don't seem to notice. When they're not eating or breeding, they just sit. Do they think? I don't know. I talked to a mountain man who walked past twenty sitting quietly in the shade. I asked: 'Were they asleep?' He said, no; apparently they felt no urge to kill him. It's a fact; they never attack a man unless he's trying to keep them from a woman, or unless they're hungry – when he'll go into the cauldron along with everything else."

"If we were carrying a bomb, we could have killed five hundred Roguskhoi," said Etzwane.

"Not a good idea," said Casallo, who tended to contest or qualify each of Etzwane's remarks. "If bombs came from balloons, they'd break the slot."

"Unless we used free balloons."

"So then? In a balloon you can only bomb what lies directly below; not often would you drift over a camp. If we had engines to move the balloons, there's a different story, but you can't build engines from withe and glass, even if someone remembered the ancient crafts."

Etzwane said, "A glider can fly where a balloon can only drift."

"On the other hand," Casallo troubled himself to point out, "a glider must land, when a balloon will drift on to safety."

"Our business is killing Roguskhoi," snapped Etzwane, "not drifting safely back and forth."

Casallo merely laughed and went off to his compartment to play his khitan, an accompliment of which he was very proud.

They had reached the heart of the Wildlands. To all sides ridges of grey rock humped into the sky; the slot veered first this way, then that, compromising between vertical and horizontal variations, the first of which made for an uneasy ride and the second for continuous exertion on the part of the winch-tender. As much as possible the slots led across the prevailing winds to afford a reach to balloons in either direction. In the mountains the winds shifted and bounced, sometimes blowing directly along the slot. The winch-tender then might luff and cant to warp his balloon off the side and low, thus minimizing the reverse vector. In worse conditions he could pull the brake cord, wedging the wheels of the dolly against the side of the slot. In conditions worse yet, when the wind roared and howled, he might abandon the idea of progress and drift back down the slot to the nearest station or siding.

Such a windstorm struck the *Iridixn* over Conceil

Cirque: a vast shallow cup lined with snow, the source of the river Mirk. The morning had shown a lavender-pink haze across the south and high in the east a hundred bands of cirrus, through which the three suns dodged and whirled to create shifting zones of pink, white, and blue. Casallo predicted wind, and before long the gusts were upon them. Casallo employed every artifice at his command: luffing, warping high and low; braking, swinging in a great arc, then releasing the brake at a precise instant to eke out a few grudging yards, whereby he hoped to reach a curve in the slot a mile ahead. Three hundred yards short of his goal the wind struck with such force as to set the frame of the *Iridixn* groaning and creaking. Casallo released the brake, put the *Iridixn* flat on the wind, and drifted back down the slot.

At Conceil Siding the station gang brought the balloon down and secured it with a net. Casallo and Etzwane rested the night in the station house, secure within a stockade of stone walls and corner towers. Etzwane learned that the Roguskhoi were very much in evidence. The size of the groups had increased remarkably during the last year, the Superintendent reported. "Before we might see twenty or thirty in a group; now they come in bands of two or three hundred, and sometimes they surround the stockade. They attacked only once, when a party of Whearn nuns were forced down by the wind. There wasn't a Roguskhoi in sight; then suddenly three hundred appeared and tried to scale the walls. We were ready for them – the area is sown thick with land mines. We killed at least two hundred of them, twenty or thirty at a time. The next day we hustled the nuns into a balloon and sent them off, and had no more trouble. Come; I'll show you something."

At the corner of the stockade a pen had been built from

49

ironwood staves; two small red-bronze creatures peered through the gaps. "We took them last week; they'd been rummaging our garbage. We strung up a net and baited it. Three tore themselves free; we took two. Already they're as strong as men."

Etzwane studied the two imps, who returned a blank stare. Were they human? derived from human stock? organisms new and strange? The questions had been raised many times, with no satisfactory answers. The Roguskhoi bone structure seemed generally that of a man, if somewhat simplified at the foot, wrist, and rib cage. Etzwane asked the Superintendent, "Are they gentle?"

"To the contrary. If you put your finger into the cage, they'll take it off."

"Do they speak, or make any sound?"

"At night they whine and groan; otherwise they remain silent. They seem little more than animals. I suppose they had best be killed, before they contrive some sort of evil."

"No, keep them safe; the Anome will want them studied. Perhaps we can learn how to control them."

The Superintendent dubiously surveyed the two imps. "I suppose anything is possible."

As soon as I return to Garwiy I will send for them, and of course you will benefit from your efforts."

"That is kind of you. I hope I can hold them secure. They grow larger by the day."

"Treat them with kindness, and try to teach them a few words."

"I'll do my best."

Down from the Wildlands drove the *Iridixn*, and across the splendid forests of Canton Whearn. For a period the wind died completely; to pass the time Etzwane watched forest birds through the binoculars: undulating air-anenomes, pale green flickers, black and lavender dragonbirds.... Late in the afternoon the wind came in a sudden rush; the *Iridixn* spun down the slot to the junction city Pelmonte.

At Pelmonte water of the river Fahalusra, diverted by flumes, provided power for six huge lumber mills. Logs floating down the Fahalusra from the forests were cleaned, trimmed, ripped into planks by saws of sintered ironweb. In seasoning yards the lumber dried in clamps, underwent surfacing, impregnation with oils, stains and special ointments then was either loaded aboard barges or cut to patterns for distant assembly. Etzwane had visited Pelmonte twice before as a Pink-Black-Azure-Deep Greener; he well remembered he redolence of raw sap, resin, varnish, and smoke which permeated the air. The canton Superintendent gave Etzwane an earnest welcome.

The Roguskhoi were well known in North Whearn; for years the lumbermen had kept a watch along the Fahalusra, turning back dozens of minor incursions, using crossbows and pikes, which in the forests were weapons more advantageous than the thrown scimitar of the Roguskhoi.

Recently the Roguskhoi had been attacking by night and in larger bands; the Whears had been driven back beyond the Fahalusra, to their great disturbance. Nowhere in Shant had Etzwane found so much zeal. The women had been sent south; the militia drilled daily. "Take this message to the Anome!" declared the Superintendent. "Tell him to send weapons! Our pikes and crossbows are futile in the open country; we need energy darts, flashing lights, death-horns, and dire contrivances. If the Anome

51

in his power and genius will provide our weapons, we will use them!"

Etzwane could find no words. The Anome, insofar as the office had meaning, was himself: a man with neither power or genius. What to say to these brave people? They should not be deceived; they deserved the truth. He said: "There are no weapons. At Garwiy the best technists of Shant are hard at work. They must be designed, tested, produced. The Anome can only do all he can."

The Superintendent, a tall harsh-faced man, cried out: "Why so tardy? He has known of the Roguskhoi for many years; why is he not ready with the means to protect us?"

"For years the Anome hoped for peace," said Etzwane. "He negotiated, he thought to contain. The Roguskhoi of course have no ears for persuasion."

"This again is no subtle or refined deduction; anyone could have seen it from the first. Now we must fight and we have none of the tools; The Anome, whatever his reasons — softness, indecisiveness, fear — has betrayed us. I say this; you may report my words; the Anome can take my head, nevertheless it is the simple wicked truth."

Etzwane gave a curt nod. "Your candour does you credit. I will tell you a secret. The Anome who so diligently hoped for peace is Anome no longer. Another man has assumed the burden and now must do everything at once. Your remarks are precisely to the point."

"I am overjoyed to hear this!" declared the Superintendent. "But in the meantime what shall we do? We have men and skill and the energy of outrage. We cannot throw ourselves away; we want to give our best: what shall we do?"

"If your crossbows kill Roguskhoi, build bigger crossbows, with greater range," said Etzwane. He remembered the Roguskhoi encampment high in the Hwan. "Build gliders: one-, two-, and six-man carriers; train flyers. Send to Haghead and Azume; demand their best gliders. Take these apart and use the pieces for patterns. For fabric and film send to Hinthe, Marestiy, Purple Stone; require their best in the name of the Anome. For cordage obtain the finest from Cathriy and Frill. In Ferriy the iron workers must set out new tanks; even though they lose their secrets, they must train new men. . . . Call on the resources of all Shant in the name of Anome."

From Pelmonte the *Iridixn* floated at speed to Luthe; from Luthe into Bleke a passenger barge towed the *Iridixn* down the Alfeis River against the sea wind. From Bleke back into Luthe the *Iridixn* drove ahead of a long-keeled coracle, which followed the river Alfeis as a dolly followed the slot. From Luthe to Eye of the East in Esterland, whence Etzwane took sailing packet to Morningshore and Ilwiy, this last canton actually in the territory assigned to Aun Sharah. Etzwane, however, thought to inspect conditions so that he might have a gauge by which to check Aun Sharah's care and accuracy.

From Ilwiy Etzwane returned to Eye of the East, again by ship. The gap in the balloon-way between Ilwiy and Eye of the East was one of several which must be closed as soon as possible! Likewise the long-planned link between Brassei in Elphine and Maschein in Maseach. The distance in each case was not great – perhaps two hundred miles – yet the balloon-way route between, in each case, extended more than sixteen hundred miles. Another loop might well be extended from Brassei west to Pagane, then through Irreale to Ferghaz at the far north of Gitanesq, then southeast through Fenesq to Garwiy. The isolated cantons Haviosq, Fordume, and Parthe had small need for balloon-way service now, true, but what of the future?

From Eye of the East the *Iridixn* drove back to Pelmonte, then swung out along the Great Southern Line, through those wild cantons fronting on the Salt Bog. In each canton Etzwane found a different situation, a different point of view. In Dithibel the women, who owned and managed all shops, refused to leave the mountain areas, out of the certain knowledge that the men would loot their stocks. At the town Houvannah Etzwane, hoarse with rage, cried: "Do you then encourage rape? Have you no sense of perspective?"

"A rape is soon; a loss of goods is long," stated the Matriarch. "Never fear, we have pungent remedies against either nuisance." But she craftily refused to spell out the remedies, merely hinting that "bad ones will rue the day. The thieves, for instance, will find themselves without fingers!"

In Burazhesq Etzwane encountered a pacifist sect, the Aglustids, whose members wore only garments fashioned from their own hair, which they argued to be natural, organic, and deleterious to no other living organism. The Aglustids celebrated vitality in its every aspect and would eat no animal flesh, no vegetable seed or kernel, no nut, and fruit only when the seed might be planted and afforded a chance to exist. The Aglustids argued that the Roguskhoi, more fecund than man, produced more life and were hence to be preferred. They called for passive resistance to "the Anome's war." "If the Anome wants war, let the Anome fight," was their slogan, and wearing their garments of matted hair they paraded through the streets of Manfred, chanting and wailing.

Etzwane was at a loss as to how to deal with them. To temporize went gainst the grain of his temperament. Still, in what direction should he act? To take the heads of so many tattered wretches was an intolerable idea: on the other hand, why should they be allowed to indulge themselves in recalcitrance while better men suffered for the common good?

In the end Etzwane threw up his hands in disgust and went his way into Shker, where he encountered a condition once more new and distinct, though with haunting echoes of the situation in Burazhesq. The Shker were diabolists, worshipping a pantheon of demons known as *golse*. They espoused an intricate and saturnine cosmology, whose precepts were based on a syllogism, thus:

Wickedness prevails throughout Durdane.
The *golse* are evidently more powerful than
their beneficent adversaries.
Therefore it becomes the part of simple
logic to appease and glorify the *golse*.

The Roguskhoi were held to be avatars of the *golse* and creatures to be revered. Arriving at the town Banily Etzwane learned that none of the Anome's orders had been heeded, much less acted upon. The Vay of Shker said with doleful fatalism: "The Anome may well take our heads; still we cannot range ourselves against creatures so sublime in their evil. Our women go willingly to them: we offer food and wine to their appetites; we make no resistance to their magnificent horror."

"This must stop," declared Etzwane.

"Never! It is the law of our lives! Must we jeopardize our future simply for your irrational whims?"

Once more Etzwane shook his head in bafflement and went on into Canton Glaiy: a region somewhat primitive, inhabited by a backward folk. They offered him no problems: the regions near the Hwan were uninhabited save for a few feudal clans, who knew nothing of the Anome's instructions. Their relationship with the Roguskhoi was not unequal; whenever possible they waylaid and killed single Roguskhoi, in order to obtain the precious metal in bludgeon and scimitar.

At the principal town, Orgala, Etzwane taxed the three High Judges with their failure to commission a militia; the Judges merely laughed. "Any time you wish a band of able men for your purposes, give us two hours' notice. Until you can provide weapons and definite orders, why should we inconvenience ourselves? The emergency may pass."

Etzwane could not dispute the logic of the remarks. "Very well," he said. "See that when the time comes you are able to perform as promised.... Where is Camp Three, the balloon-way's work agency?"

The Judges looked at him curiously. "What will you do at Camp Three?"

"I have certain orders from the Anome."

The Judges looked at each other and shrugged. "Camp Three is twenty-five miles south, along the Salt Bog Road. You plan to use your fine balloon?"

"Naturally; why should I walk?"

"No reason, but you must hire a tow of pacers; there is no slot."

An hour later Etzwane and Casallo in the *Iridixn* set forth to the south. The balloon guys were attached to the ends of a long pole, which counteracted the buoyancy of the balloon. One end of the pole was attached to the backs of two pacers; the other end was supported by a pair of light wheels, with a seat on which the driver rode. The pacers set off down the road at a fast trot, with Casallo adjusting the aspect of the balloon to produce as little strain as possible. The ride was noticeably different from the movement of a balloon on the wind, a rhythmic impulse being communicated up the guys to the balloon.

The motion and a growing tension – or perhaps he felt guilt? By dint of no great effort he might have come sooner to Camp Three – put Etzwane into a dour, dyspeptic mood. The airy Casallo, with no concerns other than the abatement of boredom, brought forth his khitan; assured of his own musicianship and Etzwane's envious admiration, he attempted a mazurka of the classical repertory which Etzwane knew in a dozen variations. Casallo played the tune woodenly and almost accurately, but on one of the modulations he consistently used an incorrect chord, which presently exasperated Etzwane to a state where he cried out in protest: "No, no, no! If you must pound that instrument, at least use the correct chords!"

Casallo raised his eyebrows in easy amusement. "My friend, you are hearing the Sunflower Blaze; it is traditionally rendered thus and so; I fear you have no ear for music."

"In rough outline, the tune is recognizable, though many times I have heard it played correctly."

Casallo languidly extended the khitan. "Be so good as to instruct me, to my vast gratitude."

Etzwane snatched the instrument, tuned the thumb-string,* which was a pinprick sharp, played the passage

---

*The five prime strings of the khitan are named for the fingers of the right hand; the four second strings have names of unknown significance: Ja, Ka, Si, La.

correctly, with perhaps unnecessary brilliance. Then, working through a second modulation, he played an inversion of the melody in a new mode; then modulating again, he performed an excited staccato improvisation upon the original strain, more or less in accordance with his mood. He struck a double-handed coda with off-beats on the scratch-box and handed the khitan back to the crestfallen Casallo. "So goes the tune, with an embellishment or two."

Casallo looked from Etzwane to the khitan, which he now sombrely hung on a peg, and set about oiling his winches. Etzwane went to stand by the observation window.

The countryside had become wild, almost hostile: patches of white and black rainforest stood like islands on a sea of saw grass. As they travelled south the jungles grew darker and denser, the saw grass showed patches of rot, and presently gave way to banks of blue-white fleshmolt. Ahead gleamed the Brunai River; the road swung somewhat away and to the west, up and across a volcanic flow of rotten grey rocks, then detoured a vast field of overgrown ruins: the city Matrice, besieged and destroyed by the Palasedrans two thousand years before, now inhabited by the huge, blue-black ahulphs of South Glaiy, who conducted their lives in a half-comic, half-horrifying travesty of human urbanity. The ruins of Matrice overlooked a peneplain of a thousand ponds and marshes; here grew the tallest osiers of Shant, in clumps thirty and forty feet tall. The workers of Camp Three cut, peeled, cured, and bundled the withe, barged it down the Brunai to Port Palas, whence coastal schooners conveyed it to the balloon factories of Purple Fan.

Far ahead appeared a dark blot, which through the binoculars became Camp Three. Within a twenty-foot high stockade Etzwane discerned a central compound, a line of work sheds, a long two-storey dormitory. To the left stood a complex of small cottages and administration offices.

The road forked; the pacer team swung towards the administration offices. A group of men came forward and, after a word with the driver, tugged the balloon guys down to sheaves anchored to concrete posts; the pacers, moving forward, drew the *Iridixn* to the ground.

Etzwane stepped from the gondola into a world of humidity and heat. Above him Etta, Sassetta, and Zael whirled through zones of colour; the air over the wasteland quivered; mirages could not be differentiated from the myriad sloughs and ponds.

Three men came slowly forward: one tall, full-fleshed, with bitter grey eyes; the second stocky, bald, with an enormous chin and jaw; the third somewhat younger, lithe and supple as a lizard, with inappropriate black ringlets and flint-black eyes. They were part with the landscape: harsh humourless men without ease or trust. They wore wide-brimmed hats of bleached saw-grass cord, white tunics, grey trousers, ankleboots of chumpa*-hide; at their belts hung small crossbows, shooting gandlewood splints. Each stared coldly at Etzwane, who could not understand the near-palpable hostility and so for a moment was taken aback. More than ever he felt his youth, his inexperience, and, above all, the precariousness of his position. He must assume control. In a neutral voice he said:

Chumpa: amphibious creatures of the Salt Bog, cousin to the ahulph, but larger, hairless, and somewhat more sluggish of habit. The chumpa, combining the subtlety and malice of the ahulph with a hysterical obstinacy, were proof against domestication.

59

"'I am Gastel Etzwane, Executive Aide to the Anome. I speak with the Anome's voice."

The first man gave a slow ambiguous nod, as if at the confirmation of a suspicion. "What brings you here to Camp Three? We are balloon-way people, responsible to balloon-way control."

Etzwane, when he sensed hostility, had developed a habit of pausing to inspect the face of his adversary: a tactic which sometimes upset the other's psychological rhythm and sometimes gave Etzwane time to choose among options. He paused now to consider the face of the man before him, and then chose to ignore the question altogether. "Who are you?"

"I am Chief Custodian of Camp Three, Shirge Hillen."

"How many men work at Camp Three?"

"Counting all personnel: two hundred and three." Hillen's tone was surly, at the very edge of truculence. He wore a torc with the balloon-way code; the balloon-way had been his life.

"How many indentured men?"

"One hundred and ninety."

"I want to inspect the camp."

The corners of Hillen's grey lips pulled back. "It is inadvisable. We have hard cases here; this is a camp for recalcitrants. Had you notified us of your coming, we would have taken proper precautions. At this moment I cannot recommend that you take your inspection. I will give you all relevant information in my office. This way, if you please."

"I must obey the Anome's instructions," said Etzwane in a matter-of-fact voice. "By the same token you must obey me or lose your head." He brought out his pulse-emitter and punched buttons. "Candidly, I do not like your attitude."

Hillen gave the brim of his hat a twitch. "What do you want to see?"

"I'll start with the work area." Etzwane looked at the other two men: the one bald and somewhat short, with immensely wide shoulders and long, knotted arms, which in some particular seemed twisted or deformed. This man's face was curiously still and composed, as if his thoughts occupied an exalted level. The other man, with the black ringlets and black eyes, was not ill-favoured, save for a long, crooked nose, which gave him a devious, dangerous look. Etzwane addressed the two to-gether: "What are your functions?"

Hillen allowed no opportunity for reply. "They are my assistants; I give orders which they carry out."

As Etzwane confronted the three men, his purposes underwent a change. Shirge Hillen apparently had received advance warning of his coming. If so – from whom, to what effect, and why? First, a precaution. Turning on his heel, Etzwane went to where Casallo lounged beside the *Iridixn*, studying a blade of saw grass. "Something is very wrong here," said Etzwane. "Take the balloon aloft; don't bring it down unless I signal with my left hand. If I'm not back before sunset, cut your guys and trust to the wind."

Casallo's aplomb was disturbed by not so much as a raised eyebrow. "Certainly; indeed; just as you wish." He turned a glance of supercilious distaste over Etzwane's shoulder. Etzwane swung around to find Hillen standing with his hand close at his dart gun, his mouth twitching. . . . Etzwane took a slow step back, to where he could now hold Casallo in view. In a sudden, frightening dazzle came a new realization: Casallo had been assigned to the *Iridixn* by officials of the balloon-way. Etzwane could trust no one. He was alone.

Best to maintain the face of trust; Casallo after all might not be party to the plot. But why had he not warned of Hillen's hand so close to his dart gun? Etzwane said in a voice of calm explication: "Be on your guard; if they kill both of us they'd blame one of the workers, and who could prove otherwise? Get into the balloon."

Casallo slowly obeyed. Etzwane watched him closely and could not read the meaning of Casallo's backward glance. Etzwane signalled the hostler: "Let the balloon go aloft." He waited until the *Iridixn* floated three hundred yards overhead, then walked back to the three men.

Hillen grunted a few words over each shoulder to his assistants, then faced Etzwane, who halted at a distance of twenty feet. To the younger of the assistants Etzwane said: "Go, if you please, to your office and bring me here the roster of workers, with the record of their indentures."

The young man looked expectantly towards Hillen, who said: "Please address yourself to me; I alone give orders to camp personnel."

"I speak with the Anome's voice," said Etzwane. "I give orders as I choose, and I must be obeyed, otherwise heads leave necks."

Hillen showed no trepidation. He gestured to his assistant. "Go fetch the records."

Etzwane spoke to the short man. "What are your duties?"

The man looked towards Hillen, his face bland and placid.

Hillen said, "He acts as my bodyguard when I walk

among the workers. We deal with desperate men at Camp Three."

"We won't need him," said Etzwane. "Go to the office and stay there until you are summoned."

Hillen made an indifferent gesture; the short man departed.

Hillen and Etzwane waited in silence, until the younger of the assistants returned with a thick grey ledger, which Etzwane took. "You may now return to the office and wait there; we will not need you."

The aide looked questioningly at Hillen, who gave his head a shake and signalled the man to the office. Etzwane watched with suddenly narrowed eyes: the two had betrayed themselves. "Just a moment," he said. "Hillen, why did you shake your head?"

For a moment Hillen was nonplussed. He shrugged. "I meant nothing particular."

Etzwane said in a measured voice: "At this moment we reach a critical phase in your life. Either you cooperate with me, to the exclusion of all else, or I will impose a harsh penalty. You have your choice; which is it to be?"

Hillen smiled a patently insincere smile. "If you are the representative of the Anome, I must obey you. But where are your credentials?"

"Here," said Etzwane, handing over a purple protocol bearing the Anome's sigil. "And here." He displayed the pulse-emitter. "Tell me, then: why did you shake your head to this man? What did you warn him against?"

"Insolence," said Hillen in a voice so neutral as to be an insult in itself.

"You were notified of my coming," said Etzwane. "Is this not correct?"

Hillen gave the brim of his hat a twitch. "No such notification reached me."

Around the corner of the stockade came a group of four men carrying rakes, shovels, and leather sacks of water. What if one threatened with his shovel and Hillen, in aiming his dart gun, struck Etzwane instead?

Etzwane, who held absolute power in Shant, was also absolutely vulnerable.

The garden gang shambled across the compound without menace. No threat here. But perhaps on another occasion?

Etzwane said, "Your dart guns are unneeded. Drop them to the ground, if you please."

Hillen growled, "To the contrary, they are constantly necessary. We live and work among desperate men."

Etzwane brought forth the broad-impulse tube, a destructive weapon of cruel potential, which exploded every torc within its range and could as easily destroy a thousand as one. "I make myself responsible for your safety, and I must see to my own. Drop the dart guns."

Hillen still hesitated.

"I will count to five," said Etzwane. "One –"

With dignity Hillen placed his weapon on the ground; his assistant followed suit. Etzwane moved back a pace or two and glanced into the ledger. Each page detailed the name of a worker, his torc code, a resumé of his background. Figures indicated the fluctuating status of his indenture.

Nowhere did Etzwane see the name *Jerd Finnerack*. Odd. "We will visit the stockade," he told Hillen. "You may return to the office." This last was for Hillen's assistant.

They marched through the afternoon glare to the tall

stockade, the portals of which stood open. Flight would have little appeal for a man in this soggy land of chumpa, blue-black ahulph, swamp vermin.

Inside the stockade the heat was concentrated and rose in shimmering waves. To one side were tanks and racks, to the other was a great shed where the withe was peeled, scraped, graded, hardened, and packed. Beyond were the dormitories the kitchens and refectory. The air smelled sour: a rancid odour which Etzwane assumed to derive from withe processing.

Etzwane went to the shed and looked along the line of tables. About fifty men worked here, with a peculiar list-less haste. They watched Etzwane and Hillen from the side of their faces.

Etzwane looked into the kitchens. Twenty cooks, busy at various tasks – peeling vegetables, scouring earthen-ware pots, boning the carcass of a grey-fleshed beast – turned aside expressionless glances which implied more than glares or hoots of derision.

Etzwane slowly returned to the centre of the com-pound, where he paused to think. The atmosphere at Camp Three was oppressive in the extreme. Still: what else could be expected? Indenture and the threat of indenture guaranteed that each man fulfilled his obligations; the system was acknowledged to be a useful social force. No denying, however, that under extreme circumstances, great hardship was the result. Etzwane asked Hillen, "Who cuts the withe?"

"Work parties go out into the thickets. When they cut their quota they come back in."

"How long have you been here yourself?"

"Fourteen years."

"What is the turnover in personnel?"

"They come, they go."

Etzwane indicated the ledger. "Few of the men seem to diminish their obligations. Ermel Gans, for instance, in four years has reduced his debt only two hundred and ten florins. How is this possible?"

"The men run up irresponsible charges at the canteen – drinking, for the most part."

"To the extent of five hundred florins?" Etzwane pointed to an entry.

"Gans committed an unruly act and was put into a disciplinary cell. After a month Gans decided to pay a fine."

"Where is the disciplinary annex?"

"It is an annex behind the stockade," Hillen's voice had taken on a rough edge.

"We will inspect this annex."

Hillen strove to keep his voice pitched in a tone of calm rationality. "This is not a good idea. We have serious disciplinary problems here. The interference of an outsider can create a turmoil."

"I am sure this is true," said Etzwane. "On the other hand, abuses, if such exist, come to light only when someone notices them."

"I am a practical man," said Hillen. "I merely enforce company regulations."

"Conceivably the regulations are unreasonable," said Etzwane. "I will inspect the annex."

Etzwane said in a stifled voice: "Get these men out into the air at once."

Hillen's face was like a stone. "What are your plans here at Camp Three?"

"You'll learn in due course. Bring the men up from those holes."

66

Hillen gave a terse order to the guards. Étzwane watched as fourteen haggard men came forth from the annex. He asked Hillen: "Why did you remove the name *Jerd Finnerack* from the roster?"

Hillen apparently had been waiting for the question. "He is no longer on the work force."

"He paid out his indenture?"

"Jerd Finnerack has been transferred to civil custody."

In a mild voice Etzwane asked, "Where is he now?"

"In criminal detention."

"And where is that?"

Hillen jerked his head towards the south. "Yonder."

"How far?"

"Two miles."

"Order a diligence."

The way to the detention house led across a dreary flat, mounded with rotting waste from the withe processing, then entered through a grove of enormous grey shagbarks. After the stockade, and in anticipation of the detention compound, the beauty of the way seemed weird and unreal. Masses of pale green foliage floated far overhead, ethereal as clouds; the cool spaces below were like grottoes. A few thin beams of sunlight impinged in a trefoil of circles upon the dust of the road: pale blue, pearl white, pink.

Etzwane broke the silence: "Have you seen Roguskhoi in the neighbourhood?"

"No."

The forest dwindled into a thicket of aspen, tape leaves, and stunted similax, the road broke out upon a soggy, black heath, steaming with aromatic vapours. Insects glinted past, whining like darts. Etzwane at first tended to flinch and duck; Hillen sat sternly erect.

They approached a low concrete structure almost windowless. "The detention house," said Hillen.

Etzwane, noticing a peculiar aliveness to his expression, became instantly suspicious. "Stop the diligence here."

Hillen turned him a burning, narrow-eyed glance. He looked in angry frustration towards the detention hall, then hunched his shoulders. Etzwane jumped quickly to the ground, now certain that Hillen had planned mischief. "Get to the ground," he said. "Walk to the hall, call forth the guards. Have them bring out Jerd Finnerack and send him here to me."

Hillen gave a fatalistic shrug; stepping down to the road, he trudged to the blockhouse, halting a few yards from the entrance. He called brusquely. From within came a short, fat man with unkempt wads of black hair hanging down past his cheeks. Hillen made a sharp, furious motion; the two looked back at Etzwane. The fat man asked a sad question; Hillen gave a terse reply. The fat man returned within.

Etzwane waited, his mind charged with tension. At Angwin Junction Finnerack had been a sturdy blond youth, mild and trusting. From sheer goodness, so it then had seemed, Finnerack had urged escape upon Etzwane and had even offered assistance. Certainly he had never envisioned Etzwane's dramatic act, which after the event had cost Finnerack dearly. Etzwane now realized that he had bought his own freedom at the cost of Finnerack's suffering.

From the house stumbled a thin, crooked man of indeterminate age. His yellow-white hair hung in snarls past his ears. Hillen jerked his thumb towards Etzwane. Finnerack turned to look, and across fifty yards Etzwane felt the hot, blue-white gaze. Slowly, painfully, as if his legs ached, Finnerack came down the road. Twenty feet behind strolled Hillen arms casually folded.

Etzwane called out sharply: "Hillen! go back to the house!"

Hillen appeared not to hear.

Etzwane pointed the pulse-emitter. "Go back!"

Hillen turned and, still holding his arms folded, went slowly back to the house. Finnerack looked back and forth, with a puzzled half-grin, then continued towards Etzwane.

Finnerack halted. "What do you want of me?"

Etzwane searched the corded brown face, seeking the placid Finnerack of old. Finnerack clearly did not recognize him. Etzwane asked, "You are the Jerd Finnerack who served at Angwin Junction?"

"I am and I did."

"How long have you been here?" Etzwane indicated the detention house.

"Five days."

"Why were you brought here?"

"So they could kill me. Why else?"

"But you are still alive."

"True."

"Who is inside?"

"Three prisoners and two keepers."

"Finnerack, you are now a free man."

"Indeed. Who are you?"

"There is a new Anome in the land of Shant. I am his executive assistant. What of the other prisoners? What are their crimes?"

69

"Three assaults on a guard. I have assaulted only twice; Hillen no longer can count to three."

Etzwane turned to consider Hillen, who hulked morosely in the shade of the detention house. "Hillen carries a dart gun under his arms, or so I suspect. Before my arrival, what was the conduct of the guards?"

"An hour ago they received a message from Camp Three and went to stand by the window with their weapons. Then you arrived. Hillen called to put me out. The rest you know."

Etzwane called to Hillen. "Order the guards outside."

Hillen spoke over his shoulder; two guards came forth, the first fat, the second tall and sallow with docked ears.

Etzwane moved a few slow paces forward. "All three of you – turn your backs and put your hands in the air."

Hillen stared woodenly, as if he had not heard. Etzwane was not deceived. Hillen calculated his chances, which were poor, from any aspect. Hillen disdainfully dropped the dart gun he had somehow managed to obtain. He turned and put his hands into the air. The two guards did likewise.

Etzwane moved somewhat closer. He told Finnerack: "First check the guards for weapons, then release the other prisoners."

Finnerack went to obey. Moments passed, silent except for the whine of insects and a few muffled sounds from within the detention house. The prisoners came forth: pallid, bony men blinking curiously towards Etzwane. "Pick up the dart gun," Etzwane told Finnerack. "Take Hillen and the guards to the cells; lock them up."

With ironic calm Finnerack signalled the three officials – gestures no doubt modelled upon those the officials themselves employed. Hillen, appreciating this, smiled grimly and walked into the detention house.

Whatever his faults, thought Etzwane, Hillen accepted adversity without loss of dignity. Today, from Hillen's point of view, had proved an adverse day indeed.

Etzwane consulted with Finnerack and the other two erstwhile prisoners, then went into the fetid detention house. His stomach jerked at the filth of the cells, in which Hillen and his minions hunched grim and disconsolate.

Etzwane spoke to Hillen: "Before arriving at Camp Three I bore you no ill will, but first you sought to thwart me, then to kill me. Beyond doubt you received instructions from another source. What was that source?"

Hillen only stared with eyes like lead balls.

Etzwane said, "You have made a bad choice." He turned away.

The fat guard, already streaming with sweat, called plaintively: "What of us?"

Etzwane spoke dispassionately, "Neither Finnerack, Jaime, nor Mermiente argues for your release. Each feels that clemency would be a mistake. Who should know better than they? Jaime and Mermiente have agreed to act as your jailers; henceforth you must deal with them."

"They will kill us; is this the justice of the Anome?"

"I don't know where justice lies," said Etzwane. "Perhaps it will come of itself, for you surely will get as much mercy as you gave."

Finnerack and Etzwane went to the diligence, Etzwane ill-at-ease and looking back over his shoulder. Where was justice indeed? Had he acted wisely and decisively? Had

71

he taken the weak, maudlin easy course? Both? Neither? He would never know.

"Hurry," said Finnerack. "Towards sunset the chumpas come up from the swamp."

Through the declining light they set out to the north. Finnerack began to study Etzwane from the side of his eyes. "Somewhere I have known you," said Finnerack. "Where? Why did you come for me?"

Sooner or later the question must be answered. Etzwane said, "Long ago you did me a service, which I finally am able to repay. This is the first reason."

In Finnerack's corded brown face the eyes glinted like blue ice.

Etzwane went on. "A new Anome has come to power. I serve as his executive assistant. I have many anxieties; I need an assistant of my own, a confederate on whom I can rely."

Finnerack spoke in a voice of awe and wonder, as if he doubted either Etzwane's sanity or his own. "You have chosen me for this position?"

"This is correct."

Finnerack gave a chuckle of wild amusement, as if his doubts were now resolved: both he and Etzwane were mad. "Why me, whom you hardly know?"

"Caprice. Perhaps I remember how you were kind to a desperate waif at Angwin."

"Ah!" The sound came up from the depths of Finnerack's soul. The amusement, the wonder were gone as if they had never existed. The bony body seemed to crouch into the seat.

"I escaped," said Etzwane. "I became a musician. A month ago the new Anome came to power and instantly called for war against the Roguskhoi. He required that I enforce this policy and I myself was given power. I learned of your condition, though I did not realize the harshness of Camp Three."

Finnerack straightened in his seat. "Can you guess your risk in telling this tale? Or my rage towards those who have made my life? Do you know what they have done to me to make me pay debts I never incurred? Do you know that I consider myself mad: an animal that has been made savage? Do you know how taut is the film that halts me from tearing you to pieces and running back to do the same for Hillen?"

"Restrain yourself," said Etzwane. "The past is the past; you are alive, and now we have work to do."

"Work?" sneered Finnerack. "Why should I work?"

"For the same reason I work: to save Shant from the Roguskhoi."

Finnerack uttered a harsh gust of laughter. "The Roguskhoi have done me no harm. Let them do as they like."

Etzwane could think of nothing to say. For a period the diligence rolled north along the road. They entered the shagbark grove, and the sunlight, now noticeably lavender, cast long green shadows.

Etzwane spoke. "Have you never thought how you would better the world, had you the power?"

"I have indeed," said Finnerack in a voice somewhat milder than before. "I would destroy those who had ravaged me: my father, Dagbolt, the wretched boy who took his freedom and made me pay the cost, the balloon-way magnates, Hillen. There are many."

"This is the voice of your anger," said Etzwane. "By destroying these people you do nothing real; the evil continues, and somewhere other Jerd Finneracks will ache to destroy you for not helping them when you had power."

"Correctly so," said Finnerack. "All men are bags of vileness, myself as well. Let the Roguskhoi kill all."

"It is foolish to be outraged by a fact of nature," Etzwane protested. "Men are as they are, on Durdane even more so. Our ancestors came here to indulge their idiosyncrasies; an excess of extravagance is our heritage. Viana Paizifiume understood this well and put torcs around our necks to tame us."

Finnerack tugged at his torc so viciously that Etzwane shrank away for fear of an explosion.

"I have not been tamed," said Finnerack. "I have only been enslaved."

"The system has faults," Etzwane agreed. "Still, across Shant the cantons keep peace and laws are obeyed. I hope to repair the faults, but first the Roguskhoi must be dealt with."

Finnerack gave only an uninterested shrug. They rode on in silence: out of the shagbark forest across the saw-grass meadow, now silent and melancholy in the twilight.

Etzwane spoke pensively, "I find myself in a peculiar position. The new Anome is a man of theories and ideals; he relies on me to make the hard decisions. I need help. I initially thought of you, who had helped me before and to whom I owed gratitude. But your attitude discourages me; perhaps I must look elsewhere. I can still give you freedom and wealth – almost anything you want."

Finnerack tugged again at the torc, which hung loosely around his taut brown neck. "You can't remove my noose; you can't give me real freedom. Wealth? Why not? I have earned it. Best of all give me the governance of Camp Three, if only for a month."

"What would you do if this were the case?" asked Etzwane, hoping to gauge the exact condition of Finnerack's mind.

"You would see a new Finnerack. He would be calm and judicious and calculate each act to an absolutely just proportion.

"Hillen now will die in a week or so, but he is far more guilty. His policy has been to goad the workers into insolence, or insubordination, or careless work, whereupon they are fined the labour of three months, or six months, or a year. No man in memory has paid off his indenture while working at Camp Three. I would keep him alive at least the month I was in power, in a cage where the men he has abused could come to look at him and speak to him. At the end of a month I would give him to the chumpas. The assistants, Hoffman and Kai, are unspeakable; they deserve the worst." Finnerack's voice began to vibrate. "They would work withe through the lye vats by day and go to the annex at night: this for the rest of their lives. They might live two or three months; who knows?"

"What of the guards?"

"There are twenty-nine guards. All are strict. Five are fair and inclined to leniency. Another ten are detached and mechanical. The others are brutes. These would go at once to the detention house and never return. The ten would go to the annex for an indefinite period – perhaps three months – and thereafter work withe for five years. The five good guards –" Finnerack knit his sun-bleached brows. "They offer a problem. They did what they could, but took no personal risks. Their guilt is not precise; nevertheless it is real. They deserve expiation – a year at working withe, then discharge without pay."

"And the indentured men?"

Finnerack looked around in surprise. "You talk of indenture? Everyone has paid ten times over. Each man goes forth free, with a bonus of ten times his original indenture."

"And who then is to cut withe?" asked Etzwane.

"I care nothing about withe," said Finnerack. "Let the magnates cut their own withe."

They rode on in silence, Etzwane reflecting that Finnerack's dispensations were not disproportionate to the conditions that had prompted them. Ahead, black on the violet dusk, stood the shape of the Camp Three stockade. The *Iridixn* floated above.

Finnerack indicated a crumble of rotten rock beside the road. "Someone waits for us."

Etzwane pulled the diligence to a halt. For a few seconds he considered. Then he brought forth the broad-impulse tube, pointed it towards the rocks, and pressed the button. A pair of explosions pounded against the evening calm.

Etzwane walked behind the rock, followed by Finnerack; they looked down at the headless bodies. Finnerack gave a grunt of disgust. "Hoffman and Kai. They are lucky men indeed."

At the entrance to the stockade Etzwane drew up the diligence. Camp Three was an outrage; justice must be done. But how? to whom? by whom? by which set of laws? Etzwane became confused and sat staring through the portal to where men stood in muttering groups.

Finnerack began to fidget and shiver and hiss through his teeth. Etzwane was reminded of Finnerack's set of judgments, which while harsh had seemed appropriate. He now discerned a principle which, he told himself, he should have apprehended before, since it formed the basic ethos of Shant.

For local grievance, local redress. For Camp Three crimes, Camp Three justice.

CHAPTER FIVE

Etzwane had gone aloft in the *Iridixn*. In fascination he looked down through binoculars into the stockade. The portal had been closed; the guards were confined in a storage shed. By the light of wall lanterns and a crackling bonfire men wandered back and forth, as if dazed. The best food the camp had to offer was spread out on tables – including all the delicacies of the commissary. The men ate as if at a banquet, regaling themselves with dried eel and the thin, sour wine Hillen had sold so dearly. Certain of the men began to grow agitated; they walked back and forth talking and gesticulating. Finnerack stood somewhat to the side; he had eaten and drunk sparingly. Outside the stockade Etzwane saw the furtive movement of dark shapes: ahulphs and chumpas, attracted by the unusual activity.

The men could eat no more; the cask of wine was dry. The men began to pound on the table and chant. Finnerack came forward; he called out; the chanting dwindled and ceased. Finnerack spoke at some length, and the crowd became dull and quiet, with restless motions of the shoulders. Then three men almost simultaneously jumped forward and in great good nature hustled Finnerack off to the side. Finnerack shook his head in disgust but said no more.

The three men held up their arms for quiet. They conversed among themselves and listened to suggestions from the crowd. Twice Finnerack thrust forward to make a passionate point, and on each occasion he was respectfully heard. It appeared to Etzwane that the differences concerned tactics rather than substance.

The colloquy became intense, with a dozen men pounding on the table at once.

Again Finnerack came forward, and his proposals halted the argument. One of the men took paper and stylus and wrote to Finnerack's dictation, while others in the crowd called out suggestions and emendations.

The bill of indictments – such it appeared to be – was complete. Finnerack once more moved aside and watched with a brooding gaze. The three men took charge of proceedings. They designated a group of five, who went to the storage shed and returned with a guard.

The crowd surged forward, but the three men spoke sternly and the crowd drew back. The guard was placed up on a table to confront the men so recently under his authority. One of the workers came forward and recited an accusation, punctuating each charge with a dramatic stab of the forefinger. Finnerack stood apart with lowering brows. Another man came forward and uttered his own complaints, and another and another. The guard stood with a twitching face. The three men spoke a verdict. The guard was dragged to the gate of the stockade and thrust outside. Two blue-black ahulphs came to take him; as they argued, a mottled grey chumpa lumbered up and dragged the guard off into the darkness.

Fourteen of the guards were brought forth from the

storage shed. Some came indolent and resigned, some glared in defiance, some hung back and jerked at the grip of the men who conveyed them, a few came hopefully smiling and jocular. Each was lifted up to stand on the table, in the full glare of the firelight, where he was judged. In one case Finnerack lunged forward to protest, pointing up towards the *Iridixn*. This man evaded the dark grounds beyond the stockade, where latecoming chumpas moaned. Instead he was directed to the long vats, where new withe steeped in a caustic solution, and forced to strip bark.

The remaining guards were brought forth and charged. One of these, after considerable debate, and with the guard pleading his own case, was thrust out into the night; the others were put to working withe.

All the guards had now been judged. Another cask of Hillen's wine was carried forth; the men drank and revelled, and jeered at the erstwhile guards who now worked withe. A few became torpid and sat lounging around the fire. The guards stripped bark and cursed the destiny which had brought them to Camp Three.

Etzwane put down the binoculars and went to his hammock. Events, he told himself hollowly, had gone about as well as could be hoped.... Somewhat after midnight he went again to look down into the stockade. The men sat around the fire, dozing or asleep. A few stood watching the guards work withe, as if they could never get enough of the spectacle. Finnerack sat hunched on a table to the side. After a few minutes Etzwane returned to his hammock.

Etzwane spent a tiresome morning cancelling indentures and signing indemnity vouchers for more or less arbitrary sums. Most of the men wanted no more withe cutting; in small groups they departed the camp and trudged north towards Orgala. About twenty agreed to remain as supervisors; their ambitions extended no farther. For years they had envied the guards their perquisites, now they could enjoy them to the utmost.

The *Iridixn* was brought down; Etzwane entered, followed by Finnerack, whom Casallo regarded with shock and fastidious dismay; for a fact Finnerack was somewhat unkempt. He had neither bathed nor changed his clothes; his hair was tangled and overlong; his smock was torn and filthy.

The *Iridixn* lifted into the air, the pacers set off to the north. Etzwane felt like a man awakening from a nightmare. Two questions occupied his mind. How many more Camp Threes existed in Shant? Who had warned Shirge Hillen of his visit?

At Orgala the *Iridixn* returned to the slot and, reaching on a fresh breeze, spun off into the north-west. Late in the following day they entered Canton Gorgash, and the morning after put down at the city Lord Benjamin's Dream. Etzwane found no fault with the Gorgash militia, though Finnerack made sardonic criticisms in regard to the pompous leadership, almost equal in numbers to the uninterested and sluggish soldiers themselves. "It is a start," said Etzwane. "They have no experience in these matters. Compared with the folk of Dithibel or Buraghesq or Shker, these folk are proceeding with intelligence and urgency."

"Perhaps so – but will they fight the Roguskhoi?"

"That we will learn when the time comes. How would you alter matters?"

"I would strip the uniforms and plumed hats from the officers and make cooks of the lot. The troops I would split into four corps and skirmish them daily against each other, to anger them and make them vicious."

Etzwane reflected that a similar process had altered a placid blond youth into the corded brown recalcitrant now in his company. "It may come to that before we're done. At the moment I'm content to see so earnest a turn-out."

Finnerack gave his jeering laugh. "When they find out what they're up against, there'll be less."

Etzwane scowled, not liking to hear his secret fears verbalized so openly. Finnerack, he thought, was by no means tactful. Additionally, he was less than a savoury travelling companion. Etzwane looked him over critically. "Time we were repairing your appearance, which at the moment is a cause for adverse comment."

"I need nothing," Finnerack muttered. "I am not a vain man."

Etzwane would not listen. "You may not be vain but you are a man. Consciously or unconsciously you are affected by your appearance. If you look untidy, unkempt, and dirty, you will presently apply the same standards to your thinking and your general mode of life."

"More of your psychological theories," growled Finnerack. Etzwane nonetheless led the way to the Baronial Arcades, where Finnerack grimly allowed himself to be shorn, barbered, bathed, manicured, and attired in fresh garments.

At last they returned to the *Iridixn*, Finnerack now a wiry, taut-muscled man with a square, deeply lined face, a head of tight bronze curls, a bright, ever-shifting gaze, a mouth clenched back in what at first view seemed a good-natured half-smile.

At Maschein, in Canton Maseach, the *Iridixn* reached the terminus of Calm Violet Sunset* Route. Casallo, allowing himself a final extravagance, swept the *Iridixn* in a great swooping arc around and into the wind, a fine flourish which pitched Etzwane and Finnerack to the floor of the gondola. A station gang drew the *Iridixn* to the landing dock. Without regret Etzwane jumped down from the gondola, followed by the unsmiling Finnerack, who had not forgiven Casallo his intemperate manoeuvre.

Etzwane bade Casallo farewell, while Finnerack stood sombrely to the side, then the two set forth into the city.

A passenger punt, which plied the many canals of Maschein, took them to the River Island Inn, which, with its terraces, gardens, arbours, and pergolas, occupied the whole of a rocky islet in the Jardeen. During his visits to Maschein as a penurious Pink-Black-Azure-Deep Greener, Etzwane had long and often gazed across the water at this most agreeable of hostelries; he now commanded a suite of four chambers giving on a private garden banked with cyclamen, blue spangle, and lurlinthe. The rooms were panelled in fine-grained wood, stained ash-green in the sleeping chambers, a delicate aelsheur* in the drawing

---

*The language of Shant discriminates between various types of sunsets. Hence:

feovhre – a calm, cloudless violet sunset.

arusch'thain – a violet sunset with horizontal apple-green clouds.

gorus'urhe – a flaring, flamboyant sunset encompassing the entire sky.

shergorszhe – as above; additionally with cumulus clouds in the east, illuminated and looking towards the west.

heizen – a situation where the sky is heavily overcast except for a ribbon of clarity at the western horizon, through which the sun sets.

Aelsheur: literally air-colour.

room, with the subtlest films of pale green, lavender, and dim blue to suggest meadows, and water vistas.

Finnerack looked around the chambers with a curled lip. He seated himself, crossed one leg over the other, stonily gazed out over the slow Jardeen. Etzwane allowed himself a small, private smile. Had the amenities at Camp Three been so superior?

In a limpid garden pool Etzwane bathed, then donned a white linen robe. Finnerack sat as before gazing out at the Jardeen. Etzwane ignored him; Finnerack would have to adjust in his own way.

Etzwane ordered an urn of frosted wine and copies of the local journals. Finnerack accepted a goblet of wine but showed no interest in the news, which was grim. Paragraphs by turns black, brown, and mustard-ochre reported that in Cantons Lor-Asphen, Bundoran, and Surrume the Roguskhoi were on the move, that Canton Shkoriy had fallen entirely under Roguskhoi control. Etzwane read:

> The Anome's policy of evacuating women to the maritime cantons is doubtless correct; the effect however has been to stir and stimulate the Roguskhoi to ever more ferocious depredations, that they may gratify their apparently insatiable lust. Where will this dreadful process end? If the Anome in his might cannot thrust the fearful hordes back from whence they came, in five years Shant will be a solid seethe of Roguskhoi. Where will they turn next? To Caraz? It must be so assumed, since the Palasedrans would not loose so fearful a weapon upon the folk of Shant without reserving for themselves a means of control.

Another article, surrounded in dark scarlet and grey, described the Maseach militia in sufficient detail that Etzwane decided to make no personal representations. With an uncomfortable grimace he read the final sentences:

> Our brave men have come together; they now familiarize themselves with military minutiae, long put aside and almost forgotten. With eagerness and hope they await the powerful weapons the Anome prepares; inspired by his majestic leadership they will smite the vicious red bandits and send them howling like scalded ahulphs.

"So they await my 'powerful weapons,' my 'majestic leadership,' " muttered Etzwane. If they knew him as he was – a bewildered musician, without competence, experience, or aptitude – they would be less sanguine. . . . His eye fell on a notice bordered in grey and ultramarine. Etzwane read:

> Last night at the Silver Samarsanda the druithine Dystar made his appearance. His meal was paid for long before he ordered it and anonymous gifts were pressed upon his uninterested attention. As usual he rewarded the company with astonishing hurusthra* and told of places where few are privileged to go. Dystar may return tonight to the Silver Samarsanda.

Etzwane read the notice a second and a third time. Recently he had thought nothing of music; now a wave of longing came over him: what had he done to himself?

Hurusthra: roughly, musical panoramas and insights.

Must he pass all his life in these sterile circumstances? Luxury, frosted wine, four-room garden suites – what were they to the life he had known with Frolitz and the Pink-Black-Azure-Deep Greeners?

Etzwane put the journal aside. In contrast to the life Finnerack had led he had been lucky. He turned to examine Finnerack, wondering what went on behind the taut brown countenance. "Finnerack!" Etzwane called out, "have you seen the news?" He handed the journal to Finnerack, who scanned the page with a scowl of unguessable import. "What are these mighty weapons the Anome is preparing?" asked Finnerack.

"To the best of my knowledge, they are non-existent."

"Without weapons, how do you expect to kill Roguskhoi?"

"The technists are at work," said Etzwane. "If weapons are forthcoming, the men will be armed. If not they must fight with dart guns, bows and arrows, dexax grenades and bombs, lances and pikes."

"The decision to fight comes tardily."

"I know this. The former Anome refused to attack the Roguskhoi, nor will he now explain his reasons."

Finnerack evinced a degree of interest. "He is not dead then?"

"No, he was deposed and replaced."

"Who performed this remarkable feat?"

Etzwane saw no reason to withhold the information. "Do you know of Earth?"

"I have heard it mentioned: the human home world."

"On Earth is an organization known as the Historical Institute, where Durdane is remembered. By chance I met a man named Ifness, a Fellow of the Historical Institute, who had come to study Durdane. Together we learned the identity of the Faceless Man and urged him to take steps against the Roguskhoi. He refused, so we deposed him and set new processes into motion."

Finnerack inspected Etzwane with glittering eyes. "An Earthman is Anome of Shant?"

"I wish he were," said Etzwane. "Unfortunately he refuses the job.... The Anome is someone else. I assist him; I myself need an assistant: perhaps yourself, if you have the will to serve Shant?"

"Shant has done me nothing but harm," said Finnerack. "I must live for myself alone."

Etzwane grew impatient. "Your bitterness is understandable, but should you not focus it more carefully? Working with me, you could help other victims. If you don't do this you become no better than Hillen, and far worse than the ordinary people, whom you despise so much. Who here in Maschein, for instance, knew of Camp Three? No one."

Finnerack shrugged and stared wooden out over the Jardeen, on which violet evening light was falling.

Etzwane presently spoke, in a voice he tried to keep even: "Tonight we dine at the Silver Samarsanda, where we will hear a great druithine."

"And what is that?"

Etzwane looked around in astonishment. Nothing could have better dramatized the scope of Finnerack's deprivation. Etzwane spoke more warmly, "A druithine is a musician who wanders alone. He may play the gastaing, or the khitan, or even the darabence, and his music is usually of high quality."

"I don't know one note of music from another," said Finnerack in a flat voice.

Etzwane controlled a new sense of impatience. "You will at least enjoy your meal; the Maseache are famous for their fine restaurants."

The Silver Samarsanda stood above the Jardeen, behind a line of tall pencil cypress; an irregular bulk of masonry, plastered and whitewashed, with a wide, many-slanted roof of mossy tiles. Beside the entrance five coloured lanterns hung in a vertical line: deep green, a dark, smokey scarlet, a gay light green, violet, and once more dark scarlet; and at the bottom, slightly to the side, a small, steady yellow lamp, the purport of all being: *Never neglect the wonder of conscious existence, which too soon comes to an end!*

Through a pair of tall timber doors Etzwane and Finnerack passed into the foyer, where a small boy served each a phial of grass wine and a morsel of crystallized fish, tokens of hospitality. A smiling maiden came forward, wearing the plum-coloured flounces of an ancient Maseach maenad; from each young man she clipped a trifle of hair and touched their chins with yorbane wax: a quaint survival of the olden times when the Maseach were notorious for their immoderate pleasures.

Etzwane and Finnerack entered the vaulted hall, still almost empty, and took a table close beside the musician's bench. A dish of sharp, bitter, pungent and salt pastilles was set before them. Partly from a malicious desire to confound Finnerack, Etzwane commanded the traditional Feast of Forty-Five Dishes, and also instructed the steward to lay out the best for Dystar, when and if he appeared.

The meal was served, one dish after another, with Finnerack at first grumbling at the smallness of the portions, which he considered over-dainty, until Etzwane reminded him that so far he had consumed only twelve of forty-five dishes.

Dish after dish was brought, conforming to the theoretical absolute of a gastronome dead four thousand years. Texture against texture, aroma contrasting with flavour, the colour and placement of each morsel to the ancient stipulation upon the ritually correct bowl, plate, or board. With each dish came a specified wine, tincture, essence, or brew. Finnerack's complaints dwindled; he became fascinated, or perhaps subdued.... At the twenty-eighth dish Dystar appeared in the entrance: a tall, spare man with well-shaped features, wearing grey trousers and a loose grey-black tunic. He stood a moment looking across the hall, then turned and made a fretful remark to the man standing behind him, Shobin the proprietor. For a moment Etzwane wondered if Dystar might not simply depart the premises, but Shobin went off to correct whatever deficiency Dystar had pointed out.... The lights in the arched alcoves near the musician's bench were bright; Dystar disliked illumination too strong or emphatic. Shobin made the adjustments; Dystar came forward, still not in the best of moods. He carried a khitan and a darabence with a green jade fingerplate; he placed these on the bench and then settled at a table only six feet from Etzwane and Finnerack. Etzwane had seen him on a single previous occasion, and had then been fascinated by Dystar's ease, strength, certainty.

The steward announced that his meal had been spoken for, to which Dystar gave an indifferent nod. Etzwane studied him sidelong, trying to read the flow of Dystar's thoughts. Here was his father, half of himself. Perhaps it was his duty to announce himself.... Dystar might

89

have a dozen sons, here and there across Shant, reflected Etzwane. The revelation might only irritate him.

The steward brought Dystar a salad of leeks in oil, the crust of a loaf, a dark sausage of meats and herbs, a jug of wine: a modest meal. Dystar had been sated with fine food, thought Etzwane; richness was no novelty to him, nor the attention of beautiful women. . . .

Dish after dish after dish. Finnerack, who perhaps never in his life had tasted good wine, had become more relaxed and examined the surroundings with a lessening of reserve.

Dystar finished half his food, pushed the rest away, and sat back, fingers around the stem of his goblet. His eyes passed across Etzwane's face; with a faint frown he looked back, as if troubled by a fleeting recollection. . . . He took up his khitan and for a moment examined it as if surprised to find such an ungainly and complicated instrument in his hands. He touched it lightly here and there, bringing all the unlikely parts into consonance, then put it aside for the darabence. He played a soft scale, adjusted whines and drones, then played a merry little jig, first with simple harmony, then with two voices, then three: a bit of virtuosity which he managed without effort or even any great interest. He put the darabence down and mused over his wine. . . .

The tables nearby were now crowded, with the most discriminating and perceptive folk of Maschein on hand to gain enlightenment.

Etzwane and Finnerack examined their thirty-ninth dish: pith of marrow tree, slivered, crisped, salted, in a pale green syrup, with a ball of purple jelly flavoured with maroes and ernice, barley sweet. The accompanying wine, a subtle quick liquid, tasted of sunlight and air. Finnerack looked doubtfully at Etzwane. "Never in my life have I eaten so much. Yet — my appetite remains."

"We must finish the forty-five dishes," said Etzwane. "Otherwise they are not allowed to accept our money, the pleasant fiction being that the cooks have incorrectly prepared the dishes, or served in a crude manner. Eat we must."

"If such be the case I am the man for it."

Dystar began to play his khitan: a soft lilt, with no obvious pattern, but as he proceeded, the ear began to anticipate and hear the pleasant corroboration. So far he had played nothing which Etzwane could not easily duplicate. ... Dystar struck a set of soft strange chords, then began to play the melody with the chords tolling below like mournful sea bells. ... Etzwane wondered as to the nature of Dystar's talent. Part, he thought, derived from ease and simplicity, part from profundity, part from a detachment which made him indifferent to his audience, part from a sleight which allowed him to play as the whim took him. Etzwane felt a pang of envy; for his part he often avoided passages whose resolution he could not foresee, knowing well the fragile distinction between felicity and fiasco. ... The music came to an end, without notable accent or emphasis, the sea gongs fading into mist. Dystar put the instrument aside. Taking up his goblet he gazed across the hall; then, as if in sudden recollection, he again lifted the khitan and tested a set of phrases. He played them again with an alteration of harmony and they became a twitching, eccentric melody. He modulated into another mode and the melody altered; effortlessly Dystar played the first and second together in wry counterpoint. For a moment he seemed to become interested in the music and bent his head over the neck of the khitan.

... He slowed the tempo, the doubled tunes became one, like a pair of coloured images joining to create the illusion of perspective. . . .

The last of the forty-five courses was served to Etzwane and Finnerack: a sour-sweet frost in shells of purple lacquer, with thimble-size goblets of Thousand Year Nectar.

Finnerack consumed the frost and tasted the nectar. His brown face seemed less gaunt; the mad, blue glitter was gone from his eyes. Suddenly he asked Etzwane: "How much must be paid for this meal?"

"I don't know. . . . Two hundred florins, I suppose."

"At Camp Three a man might not reduce his indenture two hundred florins in a year." Finnerack seemed rueful rather than angry.

"The system is archaic," said Etzwane. "The Anome will make changes. There will be no more Camp Threes, or Angwin Junctions, for that matter."

Finnerack turned him a glance of dour appraisal. "You seem very sure of the Anome's intentions."

For want of an appropriate reply, Etzwane let the remark go by. He raised a finger to the steward, who brought a tall earthenware flask, velvet with dust, from which he poured a cool pale wine, soft as water.

Etzwane drank; Finnerack cautiously followed suit.

Etzwane made an oblique reference to Finnerack's remark. "The new Anome in my opinion is not a man hidebound by tradition. After the Roguskhoi are destroyed important changes will be made."

"Bah!" said Finnerack. "The Roguskhoi are no great problem; the Anome need only hurl the might of Shant against them."

Etzwane chuckled sadly. "What might? Shant is feeble

as a baby. The last Anome turned his face away from danger. It is all very mysterious; he is neither a wicked nor a stupid man."

"No mystery," said Finnerack. "He enjoyed ease above exertion."

"I might agree," said Etzwane, "were there not other mysteries as well: the Roguskhoi themselves, in the first instance."

"Again no mystery: they derive from Palasedran malice."

"Hmm ... Who informed Hillen of my coming? Who gave orders that I be killed?"

"Is there any doubt? The balloon-way magnates!"

"Possible again. But there are other mysteries less easily explained." Etzwane recalled the Benevolence Garstang's suicidal attack and the peculiar mutilation worked upon his corpse, as if a rat had gnawed a hole in his chest."

Someone sat at their table. It was Dystar. "I have been studying your face," he told Etzwane. "It is a face I know, from the far past."

Etzwane collected his thoughts. "I have heard you play at Brassei; there perhaps you chanced to notice me."

Dystar glanced at Etzwane's torc to read the locality code. "Bastern, a strange canton."

"The Chilites no longer worship Galexis," said Etzwane. "Bastern is not so strange as before." Dystar, he noted, wore the rose and dull blue of Shkoriy. He asked, "Will you share our wine?"

Dystar gave a polite acquiescence. Etzwane signalled the steward, who brought another diorite goblet: eggshell thin, polished to the colour and sheen of pewter. Etzwane poured. Dystar raised a finger. "Enough ... I no longer enjoy food or wine. An innate fault, I suppose."

Finnerack gave his sudden harsh laugh; Dystar glanced at him with curiosity. Etzwane said, "For long years my friend has laboured under indenture at a camp for recalcitrants, and has known bitter times. Like yourself, he has no taste for fine food or wine, but for exactly opposite reasons."

Dystar smiled; his face a winter landscape suddenly illuminated by a shaft of sunlight. "Surfeit is not my enemy. I am troubled, rather, by what I would term an aversion to purchased pleasure."

"I am glad it is for sale," grumbled Finnerack. "I would find little elsewhere."

Etzwane looked ruefully at the expensive flask of wine. "How then do you spend your money?"

"Foolishly," said Dystar. "Last year I bought land in Shkoriy: a high valley with an orchard, a pond, and a cottage, where I thought to pass my senility. . . . Such is the folly of foresight."

Finnerack tasted the wine, put the goblet down, and looked off across the hall.

Etzwane began to feel uncomfortable. A hundred times he had envisioned the meeting between Dystar and himself, always in dramatic terms. Now they sat at the same table and the occasion was suffocated in dullness. What could he say? "Dystar! You are my father; in my face you see your own!" Bathos. In desperation Etzwane said, "At Brassei your mood was better than tonight; I recall that you played with zest."

Dystar gave him a quick glance. "Is the situation so evident? Tonight I am stale; I have been distracted by events."

"The trouble in Shkoriy?"

Dystar was silent for a moment, then nodded. "The savages have taken my valley, where I often went, where nothing ever changed." He smiled. "A mood of melancholy induces music; on occasions of real tragedy I become merely insipid. . . . By repute I am a man who plays only by caprice. Still, here are two hundred people come to listen, and I would not wish to disappoint them."

Finnerack, now drunk, his mouth sagging in a crooked smile, said, "My friend Etzwane professes musicianship; you should press him into service."

" 'Etzwane'? The master musician of old Azume," said Dystar. "Do you know this?"

Etzwane nodded. "My mother lived on Rhododendron Way. I was born nameless and took the name 'Gastel Etzwane' for my own."

Dystar reflected a moment, perhaps occupied with his own recollections of Rhododendron Way. Too long ago, thought Etzwane; he would remember nothing.

"I must perform." Dystar moved back to his bench. He took up the darabence to play a somewhat trivial set of melodies, as might be heard in the Morningshore dancehalls. Just as Etzwane began to lose interest, Dystar altered the set of his blare valve to construct a sudden new environment: the same melodies, the same rhythm, but now they told a disturbed tale of callous departures and mocking laughter, of roof demons and storm birds. Dystar muted the whines, throttled the valves, and slowed his tempo. The music asserted the fragility of everything pleasant and bright, the triumph of darkness, and ended in a dismal twanging chord. . . . A pause, then a sudden coda remarking that, on the other hand, matters might easily be quite the reverse.

Dystar rested a moment. He struck a few chords, then

played a complicated antiphony: glissandos swooping above a placid melody. His expression was abstracted, his hands moved without effort. Etzwane thought that the music came from calculation rather than emotion. Finnerack's eyelids were drooping; he had taken too much food and wine. Etzwane called the steward and paid the score; then he and Finnerack departed the Silver Samarsanda and returned to the River Island Inn.

Etzwane went out into the garden and stood in the quiet, looking up at the Schiafarilla, behind which, according to legend, lay old Earth.... When he returned to the drawing room, Finnerack had gone to his couch. Etzwane took a stylus and on a card wrote a careful message, upon which he impressed the sigil of the Anome.

He summoned a boy. "Take this message to the Silver Samarsanda, deliver it into the hands of Dystar the druithine, none other. Do not respond to any questions: give over the message and depart. Do you understand?"

"I do." The boy took the message and went off, and presently Etzwane went to his own couch.... As for the Repast of Forty-Five Dishes, he doubted if ever again he would dine so lavishly.

CHAPTER SIX

Prompted by doubt and uneasiness, Etzwane decided to pass by the cantons of the far west and return at once to Garwiy. He had been gone longer than he intended; in Garwiy events moved faster than elsewhere in Shant.

There was no balloon-way link between Maschein and Brassei, by reason of adverse winds and poor terrain, but the Jardeen River served almost as well. Rather than await the scheduled riverboat, Etzwane chartered a swift pinnace, with two lateen sails and a crew of ten to man sweeps or haul on the towrope in case of necessity.

East on a great loop through the sylvan foothills of Lor Ault they sailed, then north down Methel Vale, with mountains rising on both sides. At Griave in Fairlea they met the Great Ridge Route of the balloon-way, only to learn that all north-bound balloons had been delayed by gales driving in from the Sualle. Continuing to Brassei Junction, they boarded the balloon *Aramaad*. The Sualle gales had waned; the Shellflower winds provided a splendid reach; the *Aramaad* spun north along the slot at a steady sixty miles an hour. Late in the afternoon they slid down the Vale of Silence, through the Jardeen Gap, and five minutes later descended to Garwiy Station.

At sunset Garwiy was at its most entrancing, with the

low light from three suns drenching the glass of the tall spires, generating colour in prodigal quantities. From all directions, high and low, on and through the pure glass slabs, the domes, bulbs, bosses, and carved ornaments, among and around the balustrades of high balconies, the ranked arches and buttresses, the crystal scrolls and prismatic columns flowed the tides of saturated colour: pure purples to charm the mind; limpid greens, dark and rich, watergreen, leaf-green, emerald; dark and light blues, with ultramarine, smalt, and the range of middle blues; reflections and after-images of scarlet, inner shadows of light which could not be named; or near surfaces the lustre of time: acrid metallic films. As Etzwane and Finnerack moved slowly east, the suns departed; the colours became clouded with pearl and quickly died. Etzwane thought: of all this ancient grandeur I am master. I can gratify each whim; I can take, I can give, I can build or lay waste. . . . He smiled, unable to accept the ideas; they were artificial and unreal.

Finnerack could never before have seen Garwiy; Etzwane wondered as to his reactions. Finnerack was at least overtly unimpressed. He had given the city a single all-encompassing glance, and thereafter appeared more interested in the urbane folk who walked Kavalesko Avenue.

At a kiosk Etzwane bought a journal. The colours black, ochre, and brown immediately struck his eyes. He read:

> From Marestiy arresting news! The militia and a band of Roguskhoi have been engaged in a battle. The savage intruders, having worked awful damage in Canton Shkoriy, which must now be reckoned to-

tally under Roguskhoi control, sent a foraging party north. At the border a Marest troop staunchly denied the intruders passage, and a battle ensued. Though greatly outnumbered, the insensate red brutes advanced. The Marest men discharged arrows, killing or at least incommoding certain of the enemy; the others pressed forward without qualm. The Marest militia, adopting flexible tactics, fell back into the forest, where their arrows and fire-wad flings denied the Roguskhoi entry. The treacherous savages returned the fire-wads to set the forest ablaze, and the militia was forced back into the open. Here they were set upon by another band of savages, assembled for just such a bloodthirsty purpose. The militia suffered many casualties, but the survivors have resolved to extract a great revenge when the Anome provides them potency. All feel certain that the detestable creatures will be defeated and driven away.

Etzwane showed the report to Finnerack, who read with half-contemptuous disinterest. Etzwane's attention meanwhile had been drawn to a box outlined in the pale blue and purple of sagacious statement:

Here are presented the remarks
of Mialambre: Octagon, the
respected High Arbiter of Wale:

The years during and immediately after the Fourth Palasedran War were decisive; during these times was forged the soul of the hero Viana Paizifiume. He has rightly been called the progenitor of modern Shant. The Hundred Years War undeniably derived from his policies; still, for all its horror, this century now seems but a shadow on the water. Paizifiume created the awful authority of the Anome and, as a logical corollary, the employment of the coded torc. It is a system beautiful in its simplicity – unequivocal rigour balanced against responsibility, economy, effectiveness – which in the main has been kind to Shant. The Anomes have been largely competent; they have honoured all their commitments – to the cantons, allowing each its traditional style; to the patricians, imposing no arbitrary restraints; to the generality, making no exorbitant demands. The previous cantonal wars and depredations have receded to the edge of memory and are currently unthinkable.

Critical minds will discover flaws in the system. Justice, a human invention, is as protean as the race itself, and varies from canton to canton. The traveller must be wary lest he contravene some unfamiliar local ordinance. I cite those unfortunate wayfarers through Canton Haviosq who, when passing a shrine, have neglected the sign of sky, stomach, and soil, to their dismay; likewise the virgins careless enough to enter Canton Shalloran without certificates. The indenture system has shortcomings; the notorious vices of Canton Glirris are inherently wrong. Still, when all is weighed, we have enjoyed many placid centuries.

If the study of human interactions could become a science, I suspect that an inviolate axiom might be discovered to this effect: *Every social disposition creates a disparity of advantages.* Further: *Every innovation designed to correct the disparities, no mat-*

ter how altruistic in concept, works only to create a new and different set of disparities.

I make this remark because the great effort which must now wrench Shant will beyond all question change our lives, in modes still unimaginable.

Etzwane looked once more to see who had formulated the piece. Mialambre: Octagon of Wale ... Finnerack demanded somewhat peevishly: "How long do you propose to stand reading in the street?"

Etzwane signalled a passing diligence. "To Sershan Palace."

Finnerack presently spoke: "We are being followed."

Etzwane looked at him in surprise. "Are you sure?"

"When you stopped to buy the journal a man in a blue cape stepped off to the side. While you read he stood with his back turned. When we walked forward he did likewise. Now a diligence follows behind."

"Interesting," said Etzwane.

The diligence turned left from Kavalesko Avenue out upon the Parade of the Chama Reyans. A diligence coming at no great distance behind turned also.

"Interesting," said Etzwane once again.

For a space they rolled along the Parade, then swung up the Metempe, a marble avenue connecting central Garwiy with the three Ushkadel terraces. Similax trees stood against the sky to cast plum-coloured gloom over the pale stone. Behind, inconspicuously, came the second diligence.

A road glanced off to the side, under tape trees and similax. Etzwane called up to the driver: "Turn here!"

The driver tapped the neck of the long-legged pacer; smartly the diligence swung to the left, under tape trees so full and supple that the foliage stroked the top of the diligence. "Stop," said Etzwane. He jumped out. "Drive forward slowly."

The diligence continued, the pacers walking. Etzwane ran back to the intersection.

Silence, except for the rustle of the tapes, then the jingle of an approaching diligence. The sound grew louder; the diligence reached the intersection, halted. A keen-featured face peered up the side road. . . . Etzwane stepped forward; the man turned him a startled look, then spoke a quick word to his driver. The diligence spun away up the Metempe.

Etzwane rejoined Finnerack, who turned him a crooked side-glance, expressing a variety of emotions: dislike, vindication, saturnine amusement, and together, in an unlikely combination, curiosity with indifference. Etzwane, at first inclined to keeping his own counsel, decided that if his plans were to have application Finnerack had best be informed as fully as possible. "The Chief Discriminator of Garwiy is disposed to intrigue. This is my supposition, at least. If I am killed he is the first to suspect."

Finnerack gave a noncommittal grunt. Etzwane looked back down the Metempe; no one seemed to be following.

The diligence turned into the Middle Way as greenspark street lamps came to life. Far around the arc of the Ushkadel they drove, past the ranked palaces of the Aesthetes, and at last came to the portal of the Sershans. A bulb of massive glass flickered pale blue and violet.* Etz-

---

*In Shant no colour could be used arbitrarily. A green gate bulb implied festivity, and in conjunction with purple or dark scarlet lustres gave hospitable welcome to all comers. Greyed golds told of mourning;

102

wane and Finnerack alighted; the diligence jingled off into the gloom.

Etzwane crossed the wide loggia, followed, at a casual stroll, by Finnerack. Etzwane stopped to listen; from within came that almost imperceptible stir which told of routine and unexcited occupation. Was that not the rasp of new fibres in a wood-horn? Etzwane grimaced; he had no real bent for intrigue, coercion, large designs. What an improbable condition that he, Gastel Etzwane, should be master of Shant! Still, better he than Finnerack – or so came a message from the under part of his mind.

Etzwane put his misgivings aside. He took Finnerack to the entrance, where in response to his signal a footman drew aside the door.

Etzwane and Finnerack stepped into the reception hall, into a magic environment of opposing vitran panels, where nymphs disported in Arcadian landscapes. Aganthe came slowly forward. He looked drawn, even a trifle unkempt, as if events had eroded his morale; he saw Etzwane with a gleam of hope. Etzwane asked, "Have affairs gone well?"

"Not well!" declared Aganthe, with a ring in his voice. "The ancient Sershan Palace has never before been so misused. The musicians play jigs and ballintrys in the Pearlweb Salon; the children swim in the garden fountain; the men have ranged their caravans along the Ancestral Parade. They tie clotheslines between the Named Trees; they strew refuse without remorse. Lord Sajarano –" Aganthe controlled his flow of words.

---

violet indicated formality and receptiveness only to intimate intrusion; blue, or blue with violet, signified withdrawal and privacy. The word *kial'etse*, the mingling of violet and blue, might be used as an epithet, for example, *ls Xhiallinen kial'etse:* the snobbish and hyperaesthetic Xhiallinens. White glow attended ritual occasions.

"Well?" Etzwane prompted. "What of Lord Sajarano?"

"Again I use candour, since this is what you require. I have often speculated that Lord Sajarano might suffer a nervous disease, and I have wondered at his odd activities. I have not recently seen Lord Sajarano and I fear a tragedy."

"Take me to the musician Frolitz," said Etzwane.

"He will be found in the Grand Parlour."

Etzwane found Frolitz drinking Wild Rose wine from a ceremonial silver mug and gloomily watching three children of the troupe, who disputed posession of a hand-illuminated geography of West Caraz. At the sight of Etzwane and Finnerack he wiped his mouth and rose to his feet. "Where have you stayed so long?"

"I have travelled a wide circuit of the south," replied Etzwane, with the diffidence of long habit. "Naturally in all haste. I hope that you have profited by your rest?"

"Such profits are brummagem," snapped Frolitz. "The troupe rusticates."

"What of Sajarano?" Etzwane asked. "Has he given you difficulty?"

"No difficulty whatever; in fact he has vanished. We have been distracted with bewilderment."

Etzwane sank into a chair. "How and when did he disappear?"

"Five days ago, from his tower. The stairs were closed off; he acted no more distrait than usual. When he was served his evening meal, the window was open; he was gone like an *eirmelrath*."*

The three went up to Sajarano's private rooms. Etzwane looked from the window. Far below spread patterns

Eirmelrath: a malicious ghost of Canton Green Stone.

of moss. "Never a mark!" declared Frolitz. "Not a bird has disturbed the lay of the growth!"

A single narrow stairs connected the tower to the lower floors. "And here sat Mielke, on these selfsame stairs, discussing affairs with an under-maid. Agreed; they were not alert to the possibility of Sajarano stepping upon them on his way to freedom; still the occasion seems remote."

"Was there a rope in the room? Could he have torn up the draperies or bed linen?"

"Even with a rope he must have disturbed the moss. The linens were intact." Frolitz jumped to his feet. Holding his arms wide, fingers clenched and quivering, he asked: "How then did he leave? I have known many strange mysteries, but none so strange as this."

Etzwane wordlessly brought forth his pulse-emitter. He encoded the colours of Sajarano's torc and touched the red "Seek" button; the instrument immediately returned the thin whine of contact. He swung the mechanism in an arc; the whine waxed, then waned. "However Sajarano escaped, he fled no great distance," said Etzwane. "He seems to be up on the Ushkadel."

With Finnerack and Frolitz, Etzwane set forth into the night. They crossed the formal garden and climbed a flight of alabaster steps, the Schiafarilla casting a pale white light to show them the way. They crossed a pavilion of smooth white glass, where the secret Sershan pageants were performed, then pushed through a dense grove of similax, giant cypress, contorted ivorywoods, which ended only when they stepped out upon High Way. The pulse-emitter took them neither right nor left, but up into the dark forest above High Way.

Frolitz began to grumble. "By training and by inclination I am a musician, not a prowler of forests, nor a searcher for creatures who chose to flit off alone, or in company."

"I am no musician," said Finnerack, staring up into the forest. "Still I think it sensible to proceed only with lanterns and weapons."

Frolitz reacted sharply to the implications latent in Finnerack's remark. "A musician knows no fear! Sometimes he takes heed of reality; is this fear? You speak like a man with his head above the clouds."

"Finnerack is no musician," said Etzwane. "This is stipulated. Still, let us go for lights and weapons."

Half an hour later they returned to High Way, with glass lanterns and antique swords of forged iron-web. Etzwane also carried the energy pistol given him by Ifness.

Sajarano of Sershan had not moved from his previous position. Three hundred yards up the Ushkadel they found his corpse, laid out on a growth of white and grey lovelace.

The three swung their lanterns; the rays jerked nervously through the shades and nooks. One at a time they turned back to the shape at their feet. Sajarano, never large nor imposing, seemed a gnomish child, with his thin legs straight, his back arched as if in pain, his fine poet's forehead thrust back into the lovelace. The jacket of violet velvet was disarranged; the bony chest was bare, displaying a ghastly, gaping wound.

Etzwane had seen such a wound before, in the body of the Benevolence Garstang, on the day following his death.

"This is not a good sight," said Frolitz.

Finnerack grunted as if to say that he had seen worse, far worse.

"The ahulphs perhaps have been here," muttered Etzwane. "They might return." He played his lantern once more through the shadows. "Best that we bury him."

With swordblades and hands they scratched a shallow grave into the mould, presently Sajarano of Sershan, erstwhile Anome of Shant, was covered away from sight.

The three trudged back down to High Way, where by common impulse they turned a final glance up the hill. They then proceeded down to Sershan Palace.

Frolitz would not pass through the great glass doors. "Gastel Etzwane," he stated, "I want no more of Sershan Palace. We have enjoyed the best of foods and liquors; we own the finest instruments in Shant. Still, let us not deceive ourselves: we are musicians, not Aesthetes, and it is time that we depart."

"Your work is done," Etzwane agreed. "Best that you return to the old ways."

"What of you?" demanded Frolitz. "Do you desert the troupe? Where will I find a replacement? Must I play your parts and my own as well?"

"I am involved against the Roguskhoi," said Etzwane, "a situation even more urgent than good balance in the troupe."

"Can't other folk kill Roguskhoi?" growled Frolitz. "Why must the musicians of Shant leap to the forefront?"

"When the Roguskhoi are gone I will rejoin the troupe, and we will play to draw the ahulphs down from the hills. Until then –"

"I will not hear this," said Frolitz. "Kill Roguskhoi during the day, if this is to your taste, but at night your place is with the troupe!"

Etzwane laughed weakly, half convinced that Frolitz' suggestion was sound. "You're off to Fontenay's?"

"At this very instant. What keeps you here?"

Etzwane looked up at the palace where Sajarano's personality pervaded every room. "Go your way to Fontenay's," said Etzwane. "Finnerack and I will be along as well."

"Spoken like a rational man!" declared Frolitz with approval. "It's not too late for a few tunes yet!" In spite of his previous declaration, he marched into the palace to rally the troupe.

Finnerack spoke in a wry voice: "A man flits from a high tower to be found with a hole in his chest, as if an ahulph had tested him with an auger. Is this how life goes in Garwiy?"

"The events are beyond my comprehension," said Etzwane, "although I have seen something similar before."

"This may be.... So now you are Anome, without challenge or qualification."

Etzwane stared coldly at Finnerack. "Why do you say that? I am not Anome."

Finnerack gave a coarse laugh. "Then why did not the Anome discover Sajarano's death five days ago? It is a grave matter. Why have you not communicated with the Anome? If he existed, you would think of nothing else; instead you argue with Frolitz and make plans to play your tunes. That Gastel Etzwane should be Anome is strange enough; that he should not be is too much to believe."

"I am not Anome," said Etzwane. "I am a desperate makeshift, a man struggling against his own deficiencies. The Anome is dead; a void exists. I must create the illusion that all is well. For a period I can do this; the cantons control themselves. But the Anome's work accumulates: petitions go unanswered, heads are not taken, crimes go unpunished; sooner or later some clever man like Aun Sharah will learn the truth. Meanwhile I am impelled to mobilize Shant against the Roguskhoi as best I can."

Finnerack gave a cynical grunt. "And who then will be Anome? The Earthman Ifness?"

"He has returned to Earth. I have two men in mind: Dystar the druithine and Mialambre: Octagon. Either might qualify."

"Hmmf . . . And how do I fit into your schemes?"

"You must guard my back. I don't want to die like Sajarano."

"Who killed him?"

Etzwane looked off into the darkness. "I don't know. Many strange events happen in Shant."

Finnerack showed his teeth in a tight grin. "I don't want to die either. You are asking me to share your risks, which obviously are large."

"True. But are we not both motivated? We equally want peace and justice for Shant."

Finnerack again gave his dour grunt; Etzwane had no more to say. They went into the palace. Aganthe came to their summons. "Master Frolitz and his troupe are leaving the palace," said Etzwane. "They will not be returning and you can put matters to rights."

Aganthe's mournful face lit up. "Good news indeed! But what of Lord Sajarano? He is nowhere in the palace. I find here a cause for concern."

"Lord Sajarano had gone forth on his travels," said Etzwane. "Lock the palace securely; make sure that no one intrudes. In a day or so I will make further arrangements."

"I live by your commands."

When they stepped forth, Frolitz and the troupe were already departing, with a rumble of wheels and jocular calls.

Etzwane and Finnerack slowly descended the Koronakhe Steps. The Schiafarilla had dropped below the Ushkadel; up had come Gorcula the Dragonfish, with the twin orange eyes, Alasen and Diandas, blazing down at Durdane. Finnerack began to look back over his shoulder. Etzwane became infected by his restiveness. "Do you see someone?"

"No."

Etzwane quickened his pace; they reached the pale expanses of Marmione Plaza; here they paused in the shadows beside the fountain. No one came behind. With somewhat more assurance they continued down Galias Avenue and presently arrived at Fontenay's Inn, on the banks of the Jardeen River.

At the side of the common room Etzwane and Finnerack consumed a supper of stewed clams, bread, and ale. Looking across the well-remembered room Etzwane was moved to reminiscence. He told of his adventures after fleeing Angwin Junction. He described the Roguskhoi raid on Bashon and the events subsequent; he spoke of his association with Ifness, the cold and competent Fellow of the Historical Institute. In this very room Etzwane had encountered the bewitching Jurjin, now, like Sajarano and Garstang, dead. "These events run black and yellow with mystery. I am fascinated and bewildered; I also fear a dreadful enlightenment."

Finnerack pulled at his chin. "I share only little of your fascination, still I risk the full scope of this enlightenment."

Etzwane felt a throb of frustration. "You now know the circumstances; what is your decision?"

Finnerack drank his ale and set the mug down with a thud: the most emphatic gesture Etzwane had yet seen him make. "I will join you and for this reason: the better to further my own ends."

"Before we go further, what are these ends?"

"You already must know. In Garwiy and elsewhere through Shant rich men live in palaces. They gained their wealth by robbing me, and others like me, of our lives. They must make restitution. It will cost them dear, but pay they shall, before I die."

Etzwane said in a voice without accent: "Your goals are understandable. For the present they must be put aside, lest they interfere with larger matters."

"The Roguskhoi are the imminent enemies," said Finnerack. "We shall drive them back to Palasedra, and then wreak an equal justice upon the magnates."

"I promise nothing so wide as this," said Etzwane. "Fair restitution, yes. Cessation of abuses, yes. Revenge – no."

"The past cannot be erased," said Finnerack woodenly.

Etzwane pressed the matter no further. For better or worse, he must make do with Finnerack, at least for the present. The future? . . . If necessary, he would be merciless. He reached into his pocket. "I now give you the instrument I took from the Benevolence Garstang. This is how to encode a torc." Etzwane demonstrated. "Mind!

here is the critical operation! First you must press 'Grey' to disarm the self-destruction cell. 'Red' is 'Seek'; 'Yellow' is 'Kill.' "

Finnerack examined the box. "I am to keep this?"

"Until I require its return."

Finnerack turned his twisted grin upon Etzwane. "What if I craved power? I need only set the code to your colour and press 'Yellow.' Then Jerd Finnerack would be Anome."

Etzwane shrugged. "I trust in your loyalty." He saw no point in explaining that his torc carried, in the place of dexax, a warning vibrator.

Finnerack scowled down at the pulse-emitter. "By accepting this, I bind myself to your schemes."

"This is the case."

"For the moment," said Finnerack, "our lives go in the same direction."

Etzwane realized that he could expect nothing better. "The man I most distrust," he said, "is the Chief Discriminator; he alone knew of my interest in Camp Three."

"What of the balloon-way officials? They would also know, and perhaps they would act."

"Unlikely," said Etzwane. "The Discriminators must often make such inquiries in the course of routine. Why should the balloon-way distinguish Jerd Finnerack from any other? Only Aun Sharah could connect me with you. Tomorrow I will reduce his scope. . . . Finally, here is Frolitz."

Frolitz saw them at once and came swaggering over to the table. "You have had a change of heart; my words are wisdom after all."

"I want no more of Sershan Palace," said Etzwane. "We think alike in this regard."

"Wise! And here comes the troupe, straggling in like dock coolies. Etzwane, to the stand."

Etzwane automatically rose to the familiar command, then sank back into his chair. "My hands are stiff as sticks. I cannot play."

"Come, come," blustered Frolitz. "I know better. Oil your joints with the guizol; Cune will use tringolet; I will play khitan."

"For a fact I have no heart for music," said Etzwane. "Not tonight."

Frolitz turned away in disgust. "Listen then! During this last month I have altered several passages; pay heed."

Etzwane sat back. From the stand came the beloved sounds of instruments being tuned, then Frolitz' instructions, one or two muttered replies. Frolitz gave a nod, a jerk of the elbow, and once again the familiar miracle: from chaos, music.

CHAPTER SEVEN

Etzwane and Finnerack took breakfast at a cafe to the side of Corporation Plaza. Finnerack had accepted funds from Etzwane and immediately purchased new garments: black boots, a smart black cape with a stiff round collar in the ancient fashion. Etzwane wondered if Finnerack's new appearance signified a change in his attitudes, or whether the appearance merely certified a previous condition.

Etzwane brought his mind back to the problems of the present. "Today we have much to do. First: we visit Aun Sharah, whose office overlooks the square. He will be deep in thought; he will have evolved many plans and discarded them all, or so I hope. He will know of our presence in Garwiy; he probably knows that we sit here now at breakfast. He might even put a bold face on the matter and come forth to meet us."

They scanned the square but saw no sign of Aun Sharah.

Etzwane said, "Set your emitter to this code." He recited the colours of Aun Sharah's torc. "Touch 'Grey' first, never forget. . . . Good. Now we are armed."

They crossed the square, entered the Jurisdictionary, mounted the steps to the Offices of the Discriminators.

As before, Aun Sharah came forth to greet Etzwane.

Today he wore a trim suit of dark ultramarine, with cloth shoes of the same colour, and a star sapphire dangled from his left ear by a short silver chain. He spoke with easy cordiality. "I have been expecting you. This I would expect to be Jerd Finnerack."

They entered Aun Sharah's office. Etzwane asked, "How long have you been back?"

"Five days." Aun Sharah reported the events of his journey; he had encountered every condition between sullen apathy and earnest effort.

"My experiences were much the same," said Etzwane. "All is about as we expected. One episode in Canton Glaiy, however, puzzles me. When I arrived at Camp Three the Chief Custodian, a certain Shirge Hillen, had anticipated my arrival and displayed considerable hostility. What could explain such behaviour?"

Aun Sharah gazed reflectively across the square. "The inquiries I made at the balloon-way offices conceivably sent alarms all the way to Camp Three. They are defensive in regard to their labour policies."

"There seems no other explanation," said Etzwane, glancing at Finnerack, who maintained a stony silence. Etzwane leaned back in his seat. "The Anome feels that he must now undertake drastic changes. He can govern a peaceful Shant; the energies of a Shant at war exceed his control; some of his authority must be delegated. He feels that a man of your competence is wasted in a position as limited as this."

Aunt Sharah made a smiling gesture. "I am a limited man in a limited position; this is my niche; I have no soaring ambitions."

Etzwane shook his head. "Never underestimate yourself; be certain that the Anome does not."

Rather curtly Aun Sharah asked, "What precisely do you plan?"

Etzwane reflected a moment. "I want you to administer the material resources of Shant: the metals, fibres, glass, wood. This is obviously a complicated business; and I would like you to take time – three or four days, even a week – to learn something about your new job."

Aun Sharah raised his eyebrows into quizzical arches. "You want me to leave here?"

"Exactly correct. As of now you are no longer Chief Discriminator, but rather Director of Material Procurement. Go home, think about your new job. Study the cantons of Shant and their products, learn what substances are in short supply and which are not. Meanwhile, I'll occupy your office; I have none of my own."

Aun Sharah asked in delicate disbelief: "You want me to leave – now?"

"Yes. Why not?"

"But – my private files . . ."

"'Private'? Affairs which do not pertain to the office of the Chief Discriminator?"

Aun Sharah's smile became a trifle wild. "Personal effects, memoranda . . . All this seems so abrupt."

"By necessity. Events are occurring abruptly; I have no time for formalities. Where is the roster of Discriminator personnel?"

"In yonder cupboard."

"It includes your unofficial operatives?"

"Not all of them."

"You have a subsidiary list?"

Aun Sharah hesitated, then reached into his pocket and brought forth a notebook. He looked into it, frowned, carefully tore out a page, and placed it on the desk. Etzwane saw a list of a dozen names, each followed by a code symbol. "These persons do what?"

"They are informal specialists, so to speak. This man informs me on poisons, this on illicit indentures; this one and this one on affairs of the Aesthetes, where, surprisingly, hidden crimes sometimes occur. These three are receivers of stolen goods."

"What of this person, for instance?"

"He is an ahulph owner; a tracker."

"And this?"

"The same. All the others as well."

"All own ahulphs?"

"My information is not so exact. Perhaps some obtain ahulphs by other means."

"But all are trackers?"

"So I believe."

"There are no other spies or trackers available for duty?"

"You have the entire roster," said Aun Sharah shortly. "I'll take a few personal adjuncts now." He jerked open a cabinet in his desk and brought forth a grey ledger, a dart gun, a decorative iron chain with an iron medallion, a few other oddments. Etzwane and Finnerack stood to the side watching. Finnerack spoke for the first time. "The ledger is a personal adjunct?"

"Yes. Confidential information."

"Confidential from the Anome?"

"Unless he is interested in exploring my private life."

Finnerack said no more.

Aun Sharah went to the door, where he paused. "The changes you are making: are they the Anome's concepts or your own?"

"They stem from the new Anome. Sajarano of Sershan is dead."

Aun Sharah gave a short laugh. "I hardly expected him to survive."

"He died by means mysterious to me and to the new Anome as well," said Etzwane evenly. "The Shant of today is a strange place."

Aun Sharah became thoughtful. He opened his mouth to speak, then closed it again. With a sudden jerk he turned away and departed the office.

Etzwane and Finnerack immediately set about exploring the cupboards and shelves. They examined the roster and puzzled over the cryptic marks which Aun Sharah had posted beside many of the names. They found large-scale maps for each canton of Shant and for the citites of Garwiy, Maschein, Brassei, Ilwiy, Carbado, Whearn, Ferghez, and Oswiy. A set of indexes listed important men of each canton, with references to a master file and more of Aun Sharah's symbols; there were likewise detailed studies of the Aesthetes of Garwiy, again with a variety of cryptic references.

"No great matter," said Etzwane. "Aun Sharah's notes will be obsolete in a year. They relate to Old Shant; we have no interest in secrets and scandals. In any event I want to reorganize the Discriminators."

"How so?"

"They are now civil and cantonal police; they also gather information elsewhere in Shant. I want to detach this last function and establish a new Shant-wide agency to provide the Anome detailed intelligence regarding all of Shant."

"It is an interesting idea. I would be glad to control such an agency."

Etzwane laughed to himself with a straight face. Finnerack was sometimes wonderfully transparent. "Our first problem is the identity of the men who followed us yesterday evening. I would like you to organize this matter, at least. Acquaint yourself with the Discriminators; call a meeting of the personnel. Stress that Aun Sharah is no longer Chief Discriminator; that all orders must now derive from me. As soon as possible I want to look over all the operatives, all the trackers official and unofficial. If I see the man, I will recognize him."

Finnerack hesitated. "All very well, but how should I proceed?"

Etzwane considered a moment. To the side of Aun Sharah's desk was a bank of buttons. Etzwane pressed the top button. At once a clerk entered the room, a man plump and anxious, no older than Etzwane himself.

Etzwane said: "The former Chief Discriminator is no longer in authority, by order of the Anome. Henceforth you will take orders only from me and from Jerd Finnerack, here beside me; do you understand?"

"I do."

"What is your name?"

"I am Thiruble Archenway, with the status of Clerk Lieutenant."

"This top button summons yourself. What of these other buttons?"

Archenway explained the function of each button, while Etzwane took notes. "I have several tasks to be accomplished at once," said Etzwane. "First, I want you to introduce Jerd Finnerack throughout the office. He will be making certain arrangements. I want you then to summon three men to me here, by authority of the Anome, as quickly as is convenient. First: Ferulfio the Master Elec-

119

trician. Second: the technist Doneis. Third: Mialambre; Octagon, Arbiter of Wale."

"As quickly as possible." Thiruble Archenway bowed to Finnerack. "Sir, please step this way. . . ."

"One moment," said Etzwane.

Archenway swung about. "Yes?"

"What are your ordinary duties?"

"Errands much like those you have just put to me. I customarily adjust the Chief Discriminator's calendar, arrange appointments, screen mail, deliver messages."

"I remind you that Aun Sharah is no longer associated with the Discriminators. I want absolutely no leakage of information, gossip, hints, or implications from this office, through you or anyone else. Perhaps you had better circulate a bulletin to this effect."

"I will do as you require."

Ferulfio the Master Electrician was a man thin and pale, with quicksilver eyes. "Ferulfio," said Etzwane, "by repute you are a man as silent as a fanshank and twice as discreet."

"That I am."

"You and I will now go to Sershan Palace; I will admit you to a room housing the former Anome's radio system. You will transfer the equipment to this office and arrange it along yonder wall."

"As you say."

Etzwane, disliking Aun Sharah's desk, ordered it removed. He brought in two green leather divans, two chairs of purple-stained woadwood, upholstered in plum-coloured leather, and a long table, upon which a pert and pretty girl file clerk, watching Etzwane sidelong, placed a bouquet of irutiane and amaryls.

Archenway came into the room. He looked this way and that. "Very pleasant; a nice change. You also need a new rug. Let me think. . . ." He paced back and forth. "A floral, perhaps the Fourth Legend, in violet and coral? Somewhat too definite, too limiting; after all, you wish to establish your own moods. Better one of the Aubry Concentrics; which are frequently delightful. The connoisseurs think them ill-proportioned, but I find this very distortion quaint and amusing. . . . Perhaps after all a Burazhesq would be best, in dark grey, thracide,* umber."

"I am agreeable," said Etzwane. "Order in such a rug. We all should work in pleasant surroundings."

"My precise philosophy!" declared Archenway, "I am sorry to say that my own office leaves something to be desired. I could work more efficiently in a situation on the front elevation, somewhat larger and lighter than my present cubbyhole."

"Are any such offices vacant?"

"Not at the moment," admitted Archenway, "I can readily recommend changes. In fact, if you will allow me, I will at this instant prepare a schedule of long overdue adjustments."

"In due course," said Etzwane. "We can't do everything at once."

"I trust that you will keep the matter in mind," said Archenway. "I am now half-stifled in gloom; the door strikes my leg every time someone opens it, and the colours, in spite of my best efforts, are stupid and depressing. . . . Meanwhile, the technist Doneis awaits your convenience."

*Thracide: a sour, intense carmine.

Etzwane swung around in astonishment. "You keep Doneis waiting while you chatter of rugs and your inclinations in offices? You'll be lucky to end up tonight with any office whatever."

In consternation Archenway hurried from the room, to return with the tall, bone-thin Doneis. Etzwane ushered the technist to a divan and seated himself opposite. "You have submitted no report," said Etzwane. "I am anxious to learn what has been accomplished."

Doneis refused to relax; he sat bolt upright on the divan. "I have submitted no report because we have achieved no reportable results. You need not remind me of the need for haste; I understand this from high to low. We do the best we can."

"Do you have nothing whatever to tell me?" demanded Etzwane. "What are your problems? Do you need money? Additional personnel? Are their problems of morale? Do you lack authority?"

Doneis raised his sparse eyebrows. "We need neither money nor further personnel, unless you can supply five dozen intensively trained persons of superlative intelligence. Problems of discipline arose at first; we are not accustomed to working together. Matters are now somewhat better. We pursue what may be a promising line of inquiry. Are you interested in the details?"

"Of course!"

"There is a long-known class of materials," said Doneis, "which emerges from the retort as an extremely dense white material of waxy and somewhat fibrous texture. We call these materials the halcoids. They show a most curious propensity. When a surge of electricity passes through them, they alter to a translucent crystalline solid, with an appreciable increment in size. In the case of Halcoid

122

Four, this increment is almost one-sixth. Not a great deal, one might think, but the change occurs instantly, and with irresistible force; indeed, if Halcoid Four is not altered under pressure, it accelerates its surface to such an extent that in effect it explodes. One of our number has recently produced Halcoid Four with its fibres parallel, and this we call Halcoid Four-One. Upon an electrical impulse Four-One expands longitudinally only, the terminal surfaces moving at remarkable speed, which at midpoint we reckon to be about one-quarter the velocity of light. It has been proposed that projectiles be formed of Halcoid Four-One. We are now performing tests, but I cannot announce even presumptive results."

Etzwane was impressed by the exposition. "What other lines do you pursue?"

"We produce arrows with dexax heads, exploded by contact; these are complicated and uncertain. We are striving to perfect this weapon, as it would prove effective at middle ranges. I can give you little more news; we have essentially only settled ourselves to our work. The ancients projected light strong enough to burn away vision, but these skills are lost; our power-pods, while durable, provide only small surges."

Etzwane displayed the energy pistol which he had obtained from Ifness. "Here is a weapon from Earth. Can you learn anything useful from it?"

Doneis scrutinized the weapon. "The workmanship is beyond our capabilities. I doubt if we could learn more than the fact of our own deterioration. Of course, we have no metals of rare and various kinds, though we do fine work with our glasses and crystals." He somewhat reluctantly returned the pistol to Etzwane. "As to another matter: military communication. Here there is no lack of capability; we are skilled in the controlled pulsing of electrical currents; we manufacture coded torcs by the thousands. But the problems are still critical. To manufacture military equipment we must commandeer the facilities and skilled workmen currently manufacturing torcs. If we simply skim the torc factories of their best, then we risk producing faulty torcs, with possibly tragic consequence."

"Is there sufficiency of torcs on storage?"

"Never; this is impractical. We use the codes of recent fatalities in the new torcs to minimize the complexity of the code. If we did not do this, the codes might extend to nine, ten, or even eleven colours: a great and obvious nuisance."

Etzwane puzzled over the problem. "Is there no other less urgent industry from which workers might be diverted?"

"None whatever."

"We have a single recourse," said Etzwane. "Torcs are of no value to dead people. Produce the radios. The young people must wait for their torcs until the Roguskhoi are destroyed."

"This is my own reading of the matter," agreed Doneis.

"One last matter," said Etzwane. "Aun Sharah has become Director of Material Procurement for all Shant. Whatever your needs, you must now consult him."

Doneis had departed. Etzwane leaned back on the divan to think. Suppose the war lasted ten years; suppose for ten years pubescent children were denied their torcs. They would then be almost his own age before they encountered adult responsibilities. Would they willingly give over their unbridled freedom? Or would a whole generation of hooligans be loosed upon the complicated structure of Shant? ... Etzwane pressed the button to summon Thiruble Archenway.... He pressed again. Into the room came the girl who had prepared the bouquet. "Where is Archenway?"

"He has stepped out for his afternoon wine. He will shortly return. Incidentally," she added in a demure voice, "a distinguished gentleman sits in the hall, and it might be that he has come to speak to the Chief Discriminator. Archenway left no instructions."

"Be good enough to show him in. Your name is what?"

"I am Dashan of the house of Szandales, a clerk in Archenway's office."

"How long have you worked in this capacity?"

"Only three months."

"Hereafter when I press the bell, you will answer. Thiruble Archenway is insufficiently alert."

"I will do my best to help your Lordship in every possible way."

As she left the room she turned a quick backward glance over her shoulder, from which much or little might be assumed, depending upon the mood of the person who looked.

Dasham of Szandales tapped at the door, then looked demurely through. "The gentleman Mialambre: Octagon, High Arbiter of Wale."

Etzwane jumped to his feet; into the room came Mialambre: a man short and sturdy, if somewhat narrow-chested, in an austere gown of grey and white. His lordly head supported a stiff brush of white hair; his gaze was intense and somewhat minatory; he did not seem a man of easy congeniality.

Dashan of Szandales waited expectantly in the doorway. Etzwane said, "Bring us refreshments, if you please." To Mialambre: Octagon he said, "Please sit down; I did not expect you so soon; I am sorry to have kept you waiting."

"You are the Chief Discriminator?" Mialambre's voice was low and harsh; his gaze probed every aspect of Etzwane's appearance.

"At the moment there is no Chief Discriminator. I am Gastel Etzwane, executive assistant to the Anome. When you talk to me, you are, in effect, face to face with the Anome."

Mialambre's gaze, if anything, became more intense. Perhaps from juridical habit, he made no effort to ease the conversation, but silently awaited Etzwane's remarks.

"Yesterday the Anome read your observations in the *Spectrum*," said Eztwane. "He was much impressed by the scope and clarity of your viewpoints."

The door opened; Dashan wheeled in a table with a pot of tea, crisp cakes, candied sea fruit, a pale green flower in a blue vase. She spoke over her shoulder to Etzwane in a confiding voice: "Archenway is pale with rage."

"I'll speak to him later. Serve our distinguished visitor his needs, if you will."

Dashan poured tea and quickly left the office.

"I will be candid," said Etzwane. "A new Anome has assumed control of Shant."

Mialambre gave a grim nod, as if certain speculations of his own had been validated. "How was the event brought about?"

"To be candid once again, coercion was used. A group

126

of persons became alarmed by the passive policy of the old Anome. A change was made; we now undertake to defend the land."

"Not an instant too soon. What do you want of me?"

"Advice, counsel, and cooperation."

Mialambre: Octagon compressed his lips. "I would wish to learn your doctrines before committing myself to such an association."

"We have no particular point of view," said Etzwane. "The war must bring changes and we want them to occur in the right direction. Conditions in Shker, Burazhesq, Dithibel, Cape might well be altered for the better."

"There you tread on uncertain ground," declared Mialambre. "The traditional basis of Shant is looseness of association. To enforce a central doctrine must alter this situation, and not necessarily for the better."

"I understand this," said Etzwane. "Problems are sure to arise; we need capable men to solve them."

"Hmmf, how many such men have you recruited?"

Etzwane sipped his tea. "They do not yet outnumber the problems."

Mialambre gave a grudging nod. "I can render a conditional acceptance. The work is challenging."

"I am pleased to hear this," said Etzwane. "My temporary headquarters is Fontenay's Inn. I would like you to join me there, and we will confer at greater length."

"Fontenay's Inn?" Mialambre's voice was more puzzled than disapproving. "Is that not a tavern by the riverbank?"

"It is."

"As you wish." Mialambre frowned. "I must now bring up a practical matter. In Wale my family, consisting

127

of seven persons, subsists upon a jurist's income, which is not high. To lay the subject bare, I need money to pay my debts, lest the sheriff put me into a state of indenture."

"Your salary will be adequate," said Etzwane. "We will discuss this tonight as well."

Etzwane found Finnerack seated at a table in the central document chamber, listening to two Discriminators of high rank. Each vied for his ear; each indicated a separate array of documents. Finnerack listened with grim patience, and upon seeing Etzwane dismissed the two with a jerk of his hand; they departed with what dignity they could muster. Finnerack said, "Aun Sharah seems to have been flexible and undemanding. These two were his second and third in command. I will use them in the Department of Urban Discrimination."

Etzwane raised his eyebrows in surprise. Finnerack apparently had taken to himself the task of reorganizing the department, an activity which would seem to exceed his instructions. Finnerack went on to detail other of his evaluations. Etzwane listened with more interest for the working of Finnerack's judgements than for the subject matter itself. Finnerack's methods were direct to the point of naïveté and, as such, must work awe upon the subtle folk of Garwiy, who could only interpret simplicity as majesty, silence as craft. Etzwane became amused. The Discriminators were a typical Garwiy institution: complicated, devious, arbitrary, a situation which Finnerack appeared to regard as a personal affront. Etzwane, a musician, almost envied Finnerack his brutal power.

Finnerack concluded his exposition. "Next you wanted to look over the roster."

"Yes," said Etzwane. "If I recognize someone, Aun Sharah's candour becomes suspect."

"It becomes worse than that," said Finnerack. He picked up one of his lists. "If you like we can start now."

None of the Discriminators presently at hand resembled the hawk-faced man Etzwane had glimpsed through the window of the diligence.

The suns had rolled low down the sky. Etzwane and Finnerack wandered across Corporation Plaza to a cafe, where they drank verbena tea and watched the folk of Garwiy idle past; and none who saw these two young men – one slight, saturnine, and dark, the other gaunt, with sun-scorched blond hair and eyes like polished turquoise – could know that the destiny of Shant lay between them. Etzwane picked up the *Spectrum* from a nearby chair. An ochre-bordered panel caught his eye. He read with a heavy sensation:

From Marestiy by radio comes a report of an engagement between the newly organized militia and a band of Roguskhoi. The savage intruders, having wreaked an awful damage upon Canton Shkority, sent a foraging party north. At Gasmal Town on the border a troop of men denied them passage and ordered their retreat. The red brutes ignored the lawful injunction and a battle ensued. The Marestiy defenders discharged arrows and slung stones, many of which caused discomfort to the enemy, and infuriated them into what one observer described as "a stampede of furious red beasts." Such intemperate conduct will never prevail against the mighty weapons being forged by the Anome; sensible of this the

Marestiy militia adopted a flexible tactic. Final events and outcome are not yet known.

"The creatures are moving," said Etzwane. "Even those who have fled towards the sea are not safe."

CHAPTER EIGHT

In the plum-coloured Garwiy evening Etzwane and Finnerack made their way under coloured lights to Fontenay's Inn. At the back table Frolitz and the troupe ate a supper of broad beans and cheese, which Etzwane and Finnerack joined.

Frolitz was in a sour mood. "Gastel Etzwane's hands are tired and worn. Since his outside activities are more important than the welfare of the troupe, I will not require him to play an instrument. If he wishes, he may rattle the histels, or snap his fingers from time to time."

Etzwane held his tongue. After the meal, when the troupe brought forth their instruments, Etzwane joined them on the stand. Frolitz struck a pose of astonishment. "What is this? The grand Gastel Etzwane favours us with his presence? We are profoundly grateful. Would you be so kind as to take up your woodhorn? Tonight I work the khitan."

Etzwane blew in the familiar old mouthcup, fingered the silver buttons of which he had once been so proud. . . . Strange how differently he felt! The hands were his own; his fingers moved of their own accord up and down the buttons, but the vantage was higher, the perspectives were longer; and he played with an almost imperceptible elongation of tension at the beat.

At the intermission Frolitz came back to the troupe in a state of excitement. "Notice the man in the far corner – can you guess who sits there in silence, without his instrument? It is the druithine Dystar!" The troupe peered at the austere silhouette, each man wondering how his music had sounded in the mind of the great druithine. Frolitz said, "I asked what he did here; he said he had come at the will of the Anome. I asked, would he play music with the troupe? He said, yes, it would be his pleasure, that our work had brought the mood upon him. So now he joins us. Etzwane, to play the gastaing; I play woodhorn."

Fordyce, standing next to Etzwane, muttered, "At last you play beside your father. And still he does not know?"

"He does not know." Etzwane took up the gastaing: an instrument of deeper tone than the khitan, with a plangent resonance which must remain under the control of the damping sleeve if the harmony were not to be overwhelmed. Unlike many musicians, Etzwane enjoyed the gastaing and the subtleties to be achieved by expert tilting and sliding of the sleeve.

The troupe took up their instruments and stood waiting on the bandstand: the conventional respect due a musician of Dystar's quality. Frolitz left the stand, went to speak to Dystar; the two returned. Dystar bowed to the musicians, and his gaze rested a thoughtful instant on Etzwane. He took Frolitz' khitan, struck a chord, bent the neck, tested the scratch-box. In accordance with his prerogatives, he started a tune, a pleasant melody, deceptively simple.

Frolitz and Mielke, on the clarion, played ground notes, careful to stay harmonically aside, with the guizol and gastaing striking unobtrusive accents.... The music proceeded; the first tune came to an end: an exercise in which each participant explored the musical surroundings. ... Dystar relaxed his position and sipped from the beaker of wine which had been placed beside him. He nodded to Frolitz, who now in his turn blew a theme into the mouthcup of his woodhorn – a gasping, rasping, sardonic statement, foreign to the fluid clarity of the instrument, which Dystar emphasized with harsh, slow strokes of the scratch-box, and the music was off and away: a polyphony melancholy·and deliberate, in which every instrument of the troupe could clearly be heard. Dystar played calmly, his invention every instant opening new perspectives into the music.... The melody broke and faltered, in a manner anticipated by all; Dystar struck out an astounding exercise, starting in the upper register, working down through a perplexing combination of chords, with only an occasional resonance of the gastaing for support; down through upper-middle and lower-middle registers, backwards and forwards, like a falling leaf; this way and that, into the lower tones, to finish with a guttural elbow at the scratch-box. On the woodhorn Frolitz blew a quaver a minor interval below, which dwindled and died into the resonance of the gastaing.

As convention demanded, Dystar now gave up his instrument and went to a table at the side of the room. The troupe sat quietly for a moment or two. Frolitz considered. With a malicious twitch of the lips he handed the khitan to Etzwane. "We now play something slow and quiet – what is that night piece of Old Morningshore? *Zitrinilla* ... Third mode. Careful, all, with the breakoff

133

from the second strain. Etzwane: the time and the statement..."

Etzwane crooked the khitan, adjusted the scratch-box. The mischievous Frolitz, he well knew, had thrust him into a position from which any sensible man must recoil: the playing of khitan after one of Dystar's most brilliant improvisations. Etzwane paused a moment to think his way through the tune. He struck a chord and played the statement at a somewhat slower tempo than usual.

The tune proceeded, wistful and melancholy, and came to its end. Frolitz blew a phrase to signal a variation at a different rhythm. Etzwane found himself playing alone, the condition he had been hoping to avoid: he must now set himself up for measure against Dystar.... He played slow chords quickly damped, creating a pattern of sound and silence which became interesting to him, and which he restated in an inversion. Resisting the temptation to embellish, he played a spare, stately music. The troupe supplied ground notes, which presently became a broad theme, swelling up like a wave over the khitan, then subsiding. Etzwane played a set of clanging disharmonic chords and a soft resolution; the music ended. Dystar rose to his feet and signalled all to his table. "Beyond question," said Dystar, "here is the first troupe of Shant. All are strong, all use the sensitivity of strength. Gastel Etzwane plays as I at his age could only have hoped to play; he has known much experience of life."

"He is an obstinate man," said Frolitz. "With an important future as a Pink-Black-Azure-Deep Greener, he meddles instead with Aesthetes and *eirmelraths* and other matters which do not concern him. My counsel goes for nought."

Etzwane said in a mild voice: "Frolitz refers to the

war against the Roguskhoi, which occupies someting of my attention."

Frolitz threw wide his arms in a gesture of vindication. "From his own mouth you have heard the words."

Dystar nodded gravely. "You have cause for concern." He turned to Etzwane. "In Maschein I spoke to you and your friend who sits yonder. Immediately thereafter I received the Anome's command to journey here to Fontenay's Inn. Are these events related?"

Frolitz looked accusingly at Etzwane. "Dystar too? Must every musician in Shant go forth against the savages before you are appeased? We strike them with our tringolets, pelt them with guizols. . . . The scheme is inept!" Signalling his troupe he stalked back to the stand.

"Frolitz' remarks are irrelevant," said Etzwane. "I am indeed involved against the Roguskhoi, but on this basis –" He explained his situation in the same terms he had used with Finnerack. "I need support from the wisest persons of Shant, and for this reason I requested that you come here."

Dystar seemed mildly amused rather than startled or awed. "So then: I am here."

A figure loomed over the table. Etzwane looked up into the bleak visage of Mialambre: Octagon. "I am puzzled by your policies," stated Mialambre. "You ask that I meet you at a tavern to discuss matters of policy; I find you drinking liquors and consorting with the tavern musicians. Is the whole affair a hoax?"

"By no means," said Etzwane. "This is Dystar, an eminent druithine, and like yourself a man of wisdom. Dystar, before you stands Mialambre: Octagon, no musician, but a jurist and a philosopher, whose assistance I have also solicited."

Mialambre seated himself somewhat stiffly. Etzwane glanced from one to the other: Dystar detached and self-contained, an observer rather than a participant; Mialambre astute, exacting, a person relating each fact of existence to every other fact by a system based on the ethos of Wale. The two, thought Etzwane, had nothing in common but integrity; each would find the other incomprehensible; yet if one became Anome he would rule the other. Which? Either? ... Etzwane, looking over his shoulder, beckoned to Finnerack, who had been standing somewhat aloofly by the wall.

Finnerack had changed to a sombre garment of black twill, tight at wrists and ankles. Without change of expression he came to the table. "Here," said Etzwane, "for all his gloom is a man of probity and competence. His name is Jerd Finnerack; he tends to energetic action. We are a disparate group, but our problems run on several levels and require disparate talents."

"This is all very well, or so I suppose," said Mialambre. "Still, I find the situation irregular and our surroundings incongruous. You deal with all of Shant rather more informally than the elders control the business of our village."

"Why not?" asked Etzwane. "The government of Shant has been and is a single man, the Anome; what could be less formal than this? The government travels with the Anome; if he sat here tonight, here would be the government."

"The system is flexible," Mialambre agreed. "How it functions in times of stress remains to be seen."

"The system depends upon the men who direct it," said Etzwane, "which is to say ourselves. Much work lies be-

136

fore us. I will tell you what so far has been done: we have mobilized militias in sixty-two cantons."

"Those not now overrun," remarked Finnerack.

"The technists of Garwiy contrive weapons; the folk of Shant at last realize that the Roguskhoi must and will be defeated. On the other side of the coin, the organization to coordinate so much effort simply does not exist. Shant is a sprawling beast with sixty-two arms and no head. The beast is helpless; it struggles and thrashes in sixty-two directions but is no match for the ahulph which gnaws at its belly."

On the stand Frolitz had taken the troupe into a muted nocturne, which he played only when he felt out of sorts.

Mialambre said: "Our deficiencies are real. Two thousand years has brought many changes. Viana Paizifiume fought the Palasedrans with a brave, even ferocious army. They wore no torcs; discipline must have been a severe problem. Even so, they dealt the Palasedrans terrible blows."

"They were men in those days," said Finnerack. "They lived like men, they fought like men, and if necessary died like men. They pursued no 'flexible tactics.'"

Mialambre nodded in dour agreement. "We shall not find their like in the Shant of today."

"Yet," mused Etzwane, "they were only men, no more and no less than ourselves."

"Not true," insisted Mialambre. "The men of old were harsh and wilful, responsible to no one but themselves. They were therefore self-reliant, and here is the 'more.' The folk today are allowed no such exercises; they trust the justice of the Anome rather than the effect of their own force. They are obedient and lawful: here the olden folk were 'less.' So we have lost and so we have gained."

"The gains have no meaning," said Finnerack, "if the Roguskhoi destroy Shant."

"This will not come to pass," Etzwane declared. "Our militias must and will strike them back!"

Finnerack uttered his harsh laugh. "How can the militia do this? Can children fight ogres? A single man inhabits Shant: the Anome. He cannot do the fighting; he must order his children forth to battle. The children are fearful; they rely on the single man and the result is preordained. Defeat! disaster! death!"

There was silence except for the slow, sad music of the nocturne.

"I suspect that you overstate your case," said Mialambre in a cautious voice. "Surely Shant cannot be totally bereft of warriors; somewhere live brave men to protect their homes, to assault and conquer."

"I met a few," said Finnerack. "Like me they worked at Camp Three. They had no fear of pain, death, or the Faceless Man; what could he do worse than what they knew? Here were warriors! Men without fear of the torc! These men were free; can you believe this? Give me a militia of such brave free man and I will conquer the Roguskhoi!"

"Unfortunately," said Etzwane, "Camp Three is no more. We can hardly torment men until they lose their fear of death."

"Is there no better way to set a man free?" cried Finnerack in a rough voice. "This instant I can tell you a better way!"

Mialambre was puzzled; Dystar wondered; only Etzwane knew Finnerack's meaning. Beyond question he referred to his torc, which he must regard the instrument of his suffering.

The group sat quietly, brooding over Finnerack's words. Presently, in a voice of idle reflection, Etzwane asked: "Suppose the torcs were taken from all your necks: what then?"

Finnerack's face was stoney; he deigned no reply.

Dystar said: "Without my torc I would be mad with joy."

Mialambre seemed astounded both by the concept and by Dystar's response. "How can this be? The torc is your representation, the signal of your responsibility to society."

"I recognize no such responsibility," said Dystar. "Responsibility is the debt of people who take. I do not take, I give. Thereafter my responsibility is gone."

"Not so," exclaimed Mialambre. "This is an egotistical fallacy! Every man alive owes a vast debt to millions – to the folk around him who provide a human ambience, to the dead heroes who gave him his thoughts, his language, his music; to the technists who built the spaceships which brought him to Durdane. The past is a precious tapestry; each man is a new thread in the continuing weave; a thread by itself is without meaning or worth."

Dystar gave generous acquiescence. "What you say is truth. I am at fault. Nonetheless, my torc is unwelcome; it coerces me to the life I would prefer to live by my own free will."

"Suppose you were Anome," asked Etzwane. "What would be your policy in this regard?"

"There would be no more torcs. People would live without fear, in freedom."

" 'Freedom'?" cried Mialambre in unaccustomed fervour. "I am as free as is possible! I act as I please, within the lawful scope. Thieves and murderers lack freedom; they may not rob and kill. The honest man's torc is his protection against such 'freedom.'"

Dystar again conceded the jurist his argument. "Still, I was born without a torc. When the Sanhredin guild-master clamped my neck, a weight came upon my spirit which has never departed."

"The weight is real," said Mialambre. "What is the alternative? Illegality and defiance. How would our laws be enforced? Through a coercive corps? Spies? Prisons? Tortures? Hypnotism? Drugs? Men without restraint are ahulphs. I declare that the flaw is not the torc; it resides in the human disposition which makes the torc necessary."

Finnerack said, "The correctness of your remarks rests upon an assumption."

"Which is?"

"You assume the altruism and good judgment of the Anome."

"True!" declared Mialambre. "For two thousand years we have had this general condition."

"The magnates will agree to this. At Camp Three we thought the reverse; and we are correct, not you. What man of justice could allow a Camp Three to exist?"

Mialambre was not daunted. "Camp Three was a carbuncle upon the private parts; filth under the rug. No system lacks its flaw. The Anome enforces only canton law; he makes no law of his own. The customs of Canton Glaiy are insensitive; perhaps this is why Camp Three was located in Glaiy. Were I Anome, would I enforce new laws upon Glaiy? A dilemma for every thoughtful man."

Etzwane said, "The argument is beside the point; at

least temporarily. The Roguskhoi are about to destroy us. There will be no more torcs, no more Anome, no more men, unless we fight with effectiveness. Our performance to date has not been good."

"The Anome is the single free man of Shant," said Finnerack. "As a free man I too would fight; an army of free men could defeat the Roguskhoi."

Mialambre said, "The idea is unrealistic, in more ways than one. In the first place, the unclamped children are years from manhood."

"Why wait?" demanded Finnerack. "We need only unclamp our warriors."

Mialambre laughed quietly. "It is not possible. Fortunately so. We would have suffered the Hundred Years War for nothing. The torcs have kept the peace. The compulsion of the torc is best; I cite you the chaos of Caraz."

"Even though manhood is lost?" demanded Finnerack. "Do you envision an infinite future of halcyon peace? The pendulum must swing. The torcs must be unclamped."

Dystar asked, "How is this to be done?"

Finnerack jerked his thumb towards Etzwane. "An Earthman taught him the sleight. He is a free man; he can do as he likes."

"Gastel Etzwane," said Dystar, "take then this torc from my neck."

The decision came to Etzwane's mind by an indirect and emotional process. "I will remove your torcs. You shall be free men like myself. Finnerack will control an army of brave free men. No further children will be clamped by torcs – if only for this reason: the torc makers now supply radios to the new militia."

Mialambre said despondently: "For better or worse, Shant enters a new time of convulsion."

141

"For better or worse," said Etzwane, "the convulsion is upon us. The force of the Anome is waning; he can no longer control the spasms. Mialambre and Dystar, you must work together. Mialambre, with such staff as you elect, you shall range Shant and correct the worst flaws: the Camp Threes, the Temple Bashons, the indenture brokers, the indenture system itself. You cannot avoid conflict and controversy; these are unavoidable. Dystar, only a great musician could do what I now require of you. Alone, or with such folk as you select, you must range Shant, to tell folk by word and by the force of music of the common heritage, the unity which must come to us, unless the Roguskhoi drive us all out into the Beljamar. The details of these operations – to correct and to unify, to bring justice and common purpose – must be yours to calculate. Now, let us go up to my chambers, where you shall all become free men like myself."

CHAPTER NINE

Days passed. Etzwane engaged a suite on the fourth level of the Roseale Hrindiana, on the east side of Corporation Plaza, three minutes walk from the Jurisdictionary. Finnerack moved in with him, but two days later took a somewhat less luxurious suite in the Pagane Towers across the plaza. The pleasures of wealth held no fascination for Finnerack; his meals were spare and simple; he drank no wines or spirits; his wardrobe consisted of four relatively plain garments, each unrelieved black. Frolitz had unceremoniously taken his troupe up into Purple Fan; Mialambre: Octagon had assembled a staff of consultants, though he had not yet overcome all his misgivings in regard to the changes he would be working upon Shant.

Etzwane argued: "Our goal is not uniformity; we quell only those institutions which victimize the helpless: grotesque theologies, indenture, the old-age houses of Cape. Where once the Anome enforced law, in the new times he becomes a source of recourse."

"If torcs are no longer used, the Anome's function changes of necessity," Mialambre noted in a dry voice. "The future is unreadable."

Dystar had gone off by himself, with words to no one.

143

Mialambre: Octagon or Dystar the druithine? Either could fulfill the office of Anome; each was deficient in the other's strength. ... Etzwane wished that he could make a quick decision and unburden himself; he had no taste for authority.

Meanwhile Finnerack reorganized the Discriminators with brutal zest. The comfortable old routines were shattered; out went the timeservers, including Thiruble Archenway; departments and bureaus were consolidated. The new Intelligence Agency was Finnerack's special interest, a situation which sometimes caused Etzwane misgivings. Consulting with Finnerack in his office, Etzwane studied the spare form, the corded face, the drooping mouth, the bright blue eyes, and wondered as to the future. Finnerack now wore no torc; Etzwane's authority extended only so far as Finnerack chose to acknowledge it.

Dashan of Szandales came into the office with a tray of refreshments. Finnerack, suddenly remembering one of his arrangements, put a question to her: "The men I required – they are here?"

"They are here." Dashan's voice was terse. She disliked Finnerack and considered herself under Etzwane's authority alone.

Finnerack, unconcerned with inconsequentialities, gave her a brisk order. "Have them marshalled into the back office; we'll be there in five minutes."

Dashan flounced from the room. Etzwane watched her go with a sad half-smile. Finnerack would be a hard man to control. To urge him to greater delicacy was time wasted. Etzwane asked: "What men are these?"

"They are the last of the men on the roster. You have seen all the rest."

Etzwane had almost forgotten Aun Sharah, who in his

present post was reassuringly far from the sources of power.

The two went to the back office. Here waited fourteen men: the trackers and spies on Aun Sharah's informal roster. Etzwane walked from man to man, trying to remember the exact contours of the face he had glimpsed through the window of the diligence: a hard straight nose, a square chin, wide flinty eyes.

In front of him stood such a man. Etzwane said, "Your name, if you please?"

"I am Ian Carle."

To the others Etzwane said, "Thank you; I require nothing more." To Carle he said, "Come, if you please, to my office."

He led the way, with Carle and Finnerack walking behind. Finnerack slid shut the door. Etzwane motioned Carle to a divan; Carle silently obeyed.

Etzwane asked, "Have you ever been in this office before?"

Carle stared Etzwane eye to eye for five seconds. He said, "I have."

Etzwane said, "I want to learn something of your previous work. My authority to ask questions comes directly from the Anome; I can show you the warrant, should you require assurance. Your own conduct is not in question."

Ian Carle gave an unemotional sign of assent.

"A short time ago," said Etzwane, "you were instructed to meet the balloon *Aramaad* at Garwiy Depot, there identify a certain man – myself as a matter of fact – and follow him to his destination. Is this true?"

Carle paused only two seconds. "This is true."

"Who gave you these instructions?"

Carle spoke in an even voice, "The then Chief Discriminator, Aun Sharah."

"Did he provide background or reason for your assignment?"

"None. This was not his habit."

"What were your exact instructions?"

"I was to follow the designated man, observe whomever he met; were I to see the tall, white-haired man of uncertain age I was to abandon Gastel Etzwane and follow the white-haired man. I was naturally to gather all supplementry information of interest."

"What was your report?"

"I informed him that the subject, obviously suspicious, had no difficulty picking me out, and attempted to make physical contact with me, which I avoided."

"What other instructions did Aun Sharah then give you?"

"He told me to station myself near Sershan Palace, to be at all times discreet, to ignore the previous subject, but to watch for the tall, white-haired man."

Etzwane sat down on the divan and glanced at Finnerack, who stood with arms clasped behind his back, eyes boring into the face of Ian Carle. Etzwane felt puzzlement. The information had been supplied; Aun Sharah's activities had been illuminated. What did Finnerack see or sense that he, Etzwane, had missed?

Etzwane asked, "What other report did you make to Aun Sharah?"

"I made no other reports. When I came with my information, Aun Sharah was no longer Chief Discriminator."

"Information?" Etzwane frowned. "What information did you bring on this occasion?"

"It was general in nature. I witnessed a grey-haired man of middle size leave Sershan Palace, whom I conceived might be the person in question. I followed him to Fontenay's Inn, where I identified him as Frolitz, a musician. I returned up Galias Avenue, passing you and this gentleman near the fountain. As I turned into Middle Way I encountered a tall, white-haired man walking eastward. He hailed a diligence and asked to be taken to the Splendour of Gebractya. I followed as rapidly as possible, but I did not find him."

"Since, have you seen either the white-haired man or Aun Sharah?"

"Neither have I seen."

From somewhere, thought Etzwane, Aun Sharah had secured a description of Ifness, in whom he had taken considerable interest. Ifness had returned to Earth; the white-haired man Ian Carle had followed presumably had been an Aesthete from one of the palaces along Middle Way.

Etzwane asked, "What garments did the tall, white-haired man wear?"

"A grey cloak, a loose grey cap."

These were Ifness' preferred garments. Etzwane asked, "Was he an Aesthete?"

"I think not; he carried himself like a man from an outer canton."

Etzwane tried to remember some particular characteristic by which Ifness could be identified. "Can you describe his face?"

"Not in detail."

"If you see him again, communicate with me at once."

"As you desire." Ian Carle departed.

Finnerack spoke caustically, "There you have Aun Sharah, Director of Material Procurement. I say, drown him tonight in the Sualle."

One of Finnerack's worst faults, reflected Etzwane, was intemperance and excessive reaction, which made dealing with him a constant struggle for moderation. "He did only what you and I would have done in his place," said Etzwane shortly. "He gathered information."

"Oh? What of the message to Shirge Hillen at Camp Three?"

"That has not been proved upon him."

"Bah. When I was a boy I worked in my father's currant patch. When I found a weed I pulled it up. I did not look at it or hope that it might become a currant plant. I dealt with the weed at once."

"First you made sure it was a weed," said Etzwane.

Finnerack shrugged and stalked from the room. Dashan of Szandales came into the room, looking back towards Finnerack's departing shape with a shudder. "That man frightens me. Does he always wear black?"

"He is a man for whom the persistence and fatefulness of black were invented." Etzwane pulled the girl down upon his lap. She set an arch moment or so, then jumped to her feet. "You are a terrible philanderer. What would my mother say if she knew how things went?"

"I am interested only in what the daughter says."

"The daughter says that a man from the Wildlands has brought you a crate of wild animals, and his beasts await you on the freight ramp."

The superintendent of the station gang at Conceil Siding had brought his Roguskhoi imps to Garwiy. He said, "It's been a month since you came through the Wildlands.

You fancied my little pets then; what of them now?"

The imps Etzwane had seen at Conceil Siding had grown a foot. They stood glaring from behind the hardwood bars of the cage. "They were never angels of delights," declared the superintendent. "Now they're well on their way to becoming true fiends. On the right stands Musel; on the left Erxter."

The two creatures stared back at Etzwane with unblinking antagonism. "Put your finger through the bars and they'll twist it off for you," said the superintendent with relish. "They're as mean as sin and no two ways about it. First I thought to treat them well and win them over. I fed them tidbits; I gave them a fine pen; I said 'chirrup,' and I whistled little tunes. I tried to teach them speech and I thought to reward good behaviour with beer. To no avail. Each attacked me tooth and nail when I gave him the option. So then I thought I'd learn the truth of the matter. I separated them, and Erxter I continued to gratify and appease. The other, poor Musel, I set about to cow. When he'd strike out at me I'd deal him a buffet. When he'd gnash at my hand I'd prod him with a stick; many the beatings he's earned and collected. Meanwhile Erxter dined on the best and slept in the shade. At the end of the experiment was there any difference in their savagery? Not a twitch; they were as before."

"Hmmf." Etzwane backed away as both came to the bars. "Do they speak; do they have words?"

"None. If they understand me they give no signal. They won't cooperate or perform the smallest task, for love or hunger. They raven up every crust I throw to them, but they'd starve rather than pull a lever to get themselves meat. Now then, fiends!" He rapped on the bars of the cage. "Wouldn't you like my ankle to chew?"

He turned back to Etzwane. "Already the rascals know the difference between the male and female! You should see them bestir themselves when a woman walks past and still so young in years. I consider it a disgrace."

Etzwane asked, "How do they recognize a woman?"

The superintendent was puzzled. "How does anyone recognize a woman?"

"For instance, if a man walked by in woman's garments, or a woman dressed as a man: what then?"

The superintendent shook his head in wonder for Etzwane's subtleties. "All this is beyond my knowledge."

"It is something which we will learn," said Etzwane.

All across Shant the placards appeared, in dark blue, scarlet, and white:

> To fight the Roguskhoi a special corps has been formed:
> ### THE BRAVE FREE MEN.
> They wear no torcs.
> If you are brave:
> If you would lose your torc:
> If you would fight for Shant:
> You are invited to join the Brave Free Men.
> The corps is elite.
> Present yourself to the agency at Garwiy City.

CHAPTER TEN

Down from the Hwan came the Roguskhoi, for the first time marching under clear and obvious leadership, to the wonder of all. Who had instructed the red savages? Even more of a mystery: from where had they derived their massive scimitars, alloyed from a dozen rare metals? Whatever the answers, the Roguskhoi thrust north at a tireless lunging lope: four companies of about two hundred warriors each. They drove into Ferriy, to send the ironmongers fleeing in a panic. Ignoring the iron-vats and tanks of precious new cultures, the Roguskhoi swept wide into Cansume. At the border the Cansume militia, one of the strongest of Shant, waited with their dexax-tipped pikes. The Roguskhoi advanced with sinister care, scimitars at the ready. On the open plain the men of Cansume had no choice but to retreat; scimitars hurled at close range would cut them apart. They moved back into the nearby village Brandvade.

To lure the Roguskhoi the militia thrust forth a crowd of frightened women, and the Roguskhoi, ignoring the bellows of their chieftains, were stimulated into an attack. They stormed the village, where, among the stone huts, their scimitars could not be hurled. Pikeheads penetrated horny red hide; dexax exploded, and within minutes fifty Roguskhoi were dead.

The Roguskhoi officers reasserted themselves; the columns drew back and continued towards Waxone, Cansume's principal city. Along the way irregular units of the militia set up ambushes, from which they fired cane arrows with negligible effect. The Roguskhoi jogged out into the melon fields before Waxone, and here they stopped short, confronted by the most imposing array the men of Shant had yet put forward. An entire regiment of militia faced them, reinforced by four hundred Brave Free Men mounted on pacers. The Brave Free Men wore uniforms after the style of the Pandamon Palace Guards: pale blue trousers with purple braid down the sides, a dark blue blouse with purple frogging, helmets of cemented glass fibres. They carried dexax-tipped pikes, a brace of hand grenades, short, heavy glaywood swords, edged with forged ironweb. The militia carried hand axes, grenades, and rectangular shields of leather and wood; they had been instructed to advance towards the Roguskhoi, protecting themselves and the cavalry from the Roguskhoi scimitars. At a range of fifty feet they would hurl their grenades, then open ranks for the charge of the Brave Free Men.

The Roguskhoi stood at one end of the melon field, glowering towards the shields of the militia. The four Roguskhoi chieftains stood to the side, distinguished from the ordinary warriors by black leather neckbands supporting bibs of chain mail. They seemed older than the troopers; their skin showed duller and darker; flaps of skin or muscle, like wattles, grew under their chins. They watched the advancing militia in mild perplexity, then uttered a set of harsh sounds; the four companies moved forward at a passionless trot. From the militia came a thin sound, and the shields quivered. The Brave Free Men behind gave hoarse shouts and the militia steadied. At a distance of a hundred yards the Roguskhoi halted and brought their scimitars down, around, and back; their muscular processes knotted and tensed. In this position the Roguskhoi were a fearsome sight. The line of the militia sagged; some reflexively hurled their grenades, which exploded halfway between the lines.

From the rear the Cansume officers, somewhat insulated, blew *Advance* on their bugles; the line of shields moved forward, step by step. The Roguskhoi likewise lunged ahead and more futile grenades were thrown. Shields on the left wing sagged, leaving the Brave Free Men without protection. For half a second they hesitated, then charged, plunging against the instant hail of scimitars, which cut down man and pacer before they had moved twenty feet. Nonetheless grenades were thrown by dying arms; Roguskhoi disappeared in dust and flame.

The rest of the line sagged but cohered. A bugle blared *Charge;* the militia, now demoralized, faltered and broke too soon; again the shields fell aside, leaving the Brave Free Men exposed to the whirling scimitars. The survivors charged; pikes struck into copper chests. Explosion! dust, fumes, stench; a melee. Bludgeons pounded; gargoyle faces scowled and bellowed; grenades lofted over the line of battle, generating explosions, fountains of dust, whirls of detached arms and legs. A hideous din rose and fell: furious bugles, Roguskhoi grunts and bellows, the wild braying of wounded pacers, the despair of dying men. . . . The dust settled. Dead were half the Roguskhoi and all the Brave Free Men. The Cansume militia fled back into Waxone. The Roguskhoi moved slowly forward; then, altering direction, turned aside into Ferriy.

Finnerack made an anguished report of the battle. "There lay the best of Shant, in a mire of black blood! When they might have drawn back, they refused; from pride they charged to their deaths. Freedom they had earned so well: to what avail?"

Etzwane was surprised by the intensity of Finnerack's grief. "We know now that our men are as brave as the men of old," said Etzwane. "All of Shant will know this as well."

Finnerack seemed not to have heard. He paced back and forth, clenching and unclenching his hands. "The militia failed. They were traitors; they would go to cut withe, had I their judgment."

Etzwane said nothing, preferring not to divert Finnerack's emotion towards himself. Finnerack never would be allowed judgment of anyone.

"We can't fight the creatures at close range," said Finnerack. "What of our technists? Where are their weapons?"

"Sit down; control your distress," said Etzwane. "I will tell you of our weapons. The technists are impeded by great forces which must be regulated. A sliver of material hurls itself at enormous speed, and thereby produces a very large recoil. For use as handweapons the slivers must be made almost invisibly thin, and to absorb the recoil a ballast is ejected to the rear. The projectiles reach the ultimate limit of cold in expanding, otherwise they would instantly destroy themselves; rather, they drive a gust of hot air ahead which augments the impact. I have seen tests of fixed cannon; up to a range of a mile the guns will be most deadly. Beyond this distance the projectile erodes to nothing.

"The guns I have seen are by no means light or compact, owing to the necessary ballast. Possibly smaller weapons can be contrived; this is not yet certain. The large weapons are possible, but these must be braced against a tree, or a great stone, or thrust-poles, and hence are not so convenient. Still progress has been made.

"In addition, we are producing most ingenious glass arrows. The heads contain an electret, which upon impact produces an electric charge, which in turn detonates a disabling or even lethal charge of dexax. The problem here, I am told, is quality control.

"Finally, we are producing rocket guns: very simple, very cheap devices. The tube is cemented glass fibre, the projectile is ballasted either with a stone cylinder or an impact-detonated charge of dexax. This is a short-range weapon; accuracy is not good.

"All in all, there is cause for optimism."

Finnerack sat stock-still. He had become a man as different from the shaggy brown creature of Camp Three as that man was from the Jerd Finnerack of Angwin Junction. His frame had filled out; he stood erect. His hair, no longer a sun-crisped mat, clung to his head in golden-bronze ringlets; his features jutted forth without compromise; the mad glare of his eyes had become a blue glitter. Finnerack was a man without warmth, humour, forgiveness, and very few social graces; he wore only the black of implacability and doom, an idiosyncrasy which had earned him the soubriquet "Black Finnerack."

Finnerack's energy was boundless. He had reorganized the Discriminators with savage disregard for old procedures, previous status, or tenure, arousing not so much resentment as astonishment and awe. The Intelligence Agency became his own; in every city of Shant he established sub-agencies, linked by radio to Garwiy. The Brave

Free Men he took even more completely to himself, and wore a Brave Free Man uniform (black rather than pale and dark blue) to the exclusion of all his other clothes.

The Brave Free Men had instantly excited the imagination of all Shant. To Garwiy came men by the hundreds, of all ages and sorts, in numbers far beyond Etzwane's capacity to de-torc. He took Ifness' machine to Doneis, who called in a team of electronic technists. Gingerly they disassembled the case to peer down at the unfamiliar components, the exact engineering, the inexhaustible power cells. Such a machine, they decided, detected electron movement and generated magnetic pulses to cancel the flow.

After numerous experiments the technists were able to duplicate the function of Ifness' mechanism, though in no such compact package. Five of the devices were installed in the basement of the Jurisdictionary; teams of functionaries worked day and night removing torcs from persons accepted into the corps of Brave Free Men. Finnerack himself screened the applicants; those whom he rejected often made a furious protest, for which Finnerack had a stock reply: "Bring me the head of a Roguskhoi and his scimitar; I'll make you a Brave Free Man." Perhaps once a week one of the rejected applicants returned contemptuously to hurl head and scimitar at his feet, whereupon Finnerack, without comment, kicked head and scimitar into a chute and took the man into the corps. Of those who attempted a Roguskhoi head and failed, no one knew the number.

Finnerack's energy was so furious that Etzwane sometimes felt himself an onlooker rather than a participant in the great events. The situation reflected the efficiency of his own leadership, he told himself. So long as affairs proceeded in a correct direction, he could make no complaint. When Etzwane put questions, Finnerack responded clearly, if tersely, seeming neither to welcome nor to resent Etzwane's interest: a fact which, if anything, increased Etzwane's uneasiness; did Finnerack consider him futile, a man whom events had overtaken and passed by?

Mialambre: Octagon had taken his Justice of Shant teams out into the cantons; Etzwane received reports of his activities from incoming intelligence despatches.

The news of Dystar was less circumstantial. Occasionally word came from some far place, always to the same effect: Dystar had come, he had played music of unimaginable grandeur, exalting all who heard, and then he had gone his way.

Finnerack had disappeared. At his rooms in the Pagane Tower, at the Jurisdictionary, at the Brave Free Men camps, Finnerack was nowhere to be found.

Three days passed before he returned. To Etzwane's questions Finnerack at first made evasive remarks, then declared that he had been "looking over the countryside, taking a rest."

Etzwane put no further questions, but he was far from satisfied. Was there a woman in Finnerack's life? Etzwane thought not. His actions were uncharacteristic. Finnerack returned to work with his old verve, but Etzwane thought him a trifle less certain, as if he had learned something to perplex or unsettle him.

Etzwane wanted to know about Finnerack's activities, but would have been forced to call on the Intelligence Agency for help, which seemed not only inappropriate but foolish.... Must he then organize a second, competing intelligence system to bring him his information? Ridiculous!

The day after Finnerack's return Etzwane visited the technist workshops along the Jardeen estuary. Doneis took him along a set of benches where the new guns were in production. "Projectiles of pure Halcoid Four-One have not proved practical," said Doneis. "They expand almost instantaneously, producing unacceptable recoil. We have tried three thousand variations, and now use a stuff which expands at about one-tenth the speed of Four-One. In consequence the weapon requires only a thirty-pound ballast. Halcoid-Prax additionally is harder and less susceptible to atmospheric friction. The new splint is still no larger than a needle. . . . Here the trigger is fitted into the stock. . . . These are the elastic bands which prevent the ballast from flying to the rear. . . . The electret is inserted; the ballast is installed. . . . The mechanism is tested. . . . Here is the firing range, where the sights are mounted. We find that the weapon has an essentially flat trajectory across its entire range which is slightly in excess of a mile. Do you care to test this gun?"

Etzwane picked up the weapon, rested it upon his shoulder. A yellow dot in the optical sights, directly in front of his eye, indicated the impact area.

"Drop the magazine into this socket, throw this clamp. When you press the trigger the ballast will strike the electret, producing an impulse which stimulates the splint. Be prepared for the recoil; brace yourself."

Etzwane peered through the lens and placed the yellow dot on the glass target. He pressed the yellow button, to feel an instant shock which thrust him backward. Down the range appeared a streak of white fire, impinging upon the now shattered target.

Etzwane put down the weapon. "How many can you produce?"

"Today we will finish only twenty, but we should soon triple this number. The principal problem is ballast. We have requisitioned metal from all Shant, but it is slow in arriving. The Director of Material Procurement informs me that he has the metal but transportation is not available. The Director of Transportation tells me to the contrary. I don't know which to believe. I any event we are not getting our metal."

"I'll take care of the matter," said Etzwane. "You'll get your metal in a hurry. Meanwhile, I have a somewhat different problem for your attention: a pair of Roguskhoi imps, probably six months to a year old, already vicious, already alert to the presence of women. I think we should learn how and why they are so stimulated, what processes are involved. In short, are they affected visually, by odour, telepathically, or how?"

"I understand precisely. The problem is one of obvious importance; I will put our biologists to work at once."

Etzwane conferred first with the Aesthete Brise, the Director of Transportation, then with Aun Sharah. As Doneis had averred, each blamed the other for the lack of massive amounts of metal in Garwiy. Etzwane went into explicit detail and concluded that the problem was one of priority. Aun Sharah had preempted the available ships to transport food to the refugee-swollen maritime cantons.

"The health of the people is important," Etzwane told Aun Sharah, "but our first concern is killing Roguskhoi, which means metal to Garwiy."

"I understand all this," Aun Sharah replied shortly.

His complacent ease had gone, his complexion had lost its smooth tone. "I do the best that I can; remember, this is not my chosen occupation."

"Is this not true of all of us? I am a musician; Mialambre is a jurist; Brise is an Aesthete; Finnerack is a withe cutter. We are all fortunate in our versatility."

"Possibly true," said Aun Sharah. "I hear you have greatly changed my old Discriminators."

"We have indeed. All Shant is changing: I hope not for the worse."

The Roguskhoi swept on through north-central and northeast Shant, roaming at will through Cansume, most of Marestiy, and large parts of Faible and Purple Stone. Three times they attempted to swim the River Maure into Green Stone; on each occasion the regional militia put forth in fishing boats to pelt the invaders with dexax grenades. In the water the Roguskhoi were helpless; men knew the exhilaration of slaughtering their previously invincible opponents. The successes, however, were not real; the Roguskhoi were insensitive both to their own losses and to the human exultation; they marched thirty miles upstream to Opalsand, where the Maure flowed only three feet deep, and crossed in force. Their intent clearly was to sweep through Green Stone, Cape, Galwand, and Glirris and grind the survivors against the Roguskhoi forces already in Azume. They would thereby destroy millions of men, capture millions of women, and control all northeast Shant – a disaster of unthinkable proportions.

Etzwane conferred with Finnerack, Brise, and SanSein, this last the nominal commander of the Brave Free Men. Approximately two thousand Brave Free Men had now been armed with halcoid guns: a corps which Finnerack had intended to dispatch through Fairlea into the Hwan foothills of Sable, to hold Seamus and Bastern and to ambush and harass the Roguskhoi as they came down from the Hwan. The northeast, so he declared, must be written off; he saw no profit in desperate halfmeasures doomed to failure. For the first time Etzwane took issue with Finnerack on a major decision; to Etzwane a lack of reaction in the north-east meant the betrayal of millions; he found the idea unacceptable. Finnerack was unmoved. "Millions must die; the war is bitter. If we are to win we must steel ourselves to death and think in terms of grand strategy rather than a series of hysterical, smallscale operations.

"The principle is correct," said Etzwane. "On the other hand, we can't let preconceived doctrine tie us in knots. Brise, what ships now lie in Shellflower Bay?"

"Small vessels, the Stonebreaker packet, a few merchantmen, fishing craft: all these mostly in Seacastle harbour."

Etzwane spread out his maps. "The Roguskhoi march north up Maure Valley. The militia will impede them with grenades and land-mines. If we land our troops by night, here at this village Thran, they can occupy this ridge above Maurmouth. Then when the Roguskhoi appear, we will deal with them."

San-Sein examined the maps. "The plan is feasible."

Finnerack grunted and turned half about in his seat.

Etzwane said to San-Sein: "March your men to Seacastle, embark upon the vessels that Brise will provide; set forth at once to the east."

"We will do our utmost; but will there be time?"

"The militia must hold three days, by any ruse and tactic. Three days of fair winds should fetch you to Thran harbour."

Forty-two pinnacles, smacks, and trawlers, each carrying thirty Brave Free Men, set forth to the relief of the northeast. San-Sein himself commanded the operation. Three days the wind held fair; on the third night the winds died, to the disgust of San-Sein, who had wished to enter the harbour by night. Dawn found the fleet still a half-mile offshore, with any conceivable advantage of stealth or surprise gone by the boards. Cursing the calm weather, San-Sein scrutinized the shore through a telescope and went suddenly rigid with consternation. The lens of the telescope showed a sinister stir invisible to the naked eye. Roguskhoi crowded the harbour-front houses of Thran village. The militia had not held. The Roguskhoi had won through to the sea, to set up an ambush of their own.

A dawn wind had come to send ripples dancing over the water. San-Sein signalled his vessels together and issued new orders.

On the freshening breeze the flotilla drove into Thran harbour; instead of tying up at the jetty or anchoring, they grounded upon the shingle. The Brave Free Men, debarking, formed a skirmish line; they slowly advanced towards the harbour-side houses, from which the Roguskhoi demon masks now peered openly.

The Roguskhoi burst forth like ants from a broken ant hill to charge the beach. They were met by a thousand streaks of incandescent air and destroyed.

By Intelligence Agency radio San-Sein reported the operation to Etzwane and Finnerack. "We lost not a man; we killed six hundred. As many more retreated to Maurmouth and up the course of the Maure. There now is no question; with the guns we can hunt down the creatures as if they were crippled ahulphs. But this is not all the story. We succeeded, but only by luck. Had we put into Thran by night, as planned, I would not be here now to report the disaster. The Roguskhoi knew of our approach; they were apprised. Who betrayed us?"

Etzwane asked, "Who knew the plans?"

"Four only: those who formed them."

Etzwane sat in cogitation; Finnerack scowled towards the diaphragm.

"I will look into the matter," said Etzwane. "Meanwhile we have saved the northeast: a cause for rejoicing. Pursue the creatures; hunt them down, but use caution; beware ambushes and narrow places. The future at last looks good."

Finnerack snorted. "You, Gastel Etzwane, are an optimist who sees only a foot in front of his nose. The Roguskhoi were sent here to destroy us; do you believe that their sponsors, and I refer to the Palasedrans, will submit so easily? The future holds only trouble."

"We shall see," said Etzwane. "I must say that never before have I been called an optimist."

While reporting the foray to Brise, Etzwane inquired as to a possible leakage of information. Brise was perplexed and indignant. "Are you asking if I informed anyone of the raid? Do you take me for a fool? The answer is an unqualified no."

"The question was a formality," said Etzwane. "To close off the matter completely, there was no arrangement or understanding between you and the Office of Material Procurement?"

Brise hesitated, then chose his words carefully. "There was absolutely no mention of a raid."

Etzwane's senses were alert to the slightest subtlety of intonation. "I see. What precisely was your discussion?"

"A trivial affair. The Director wanted ships sent to Oswiy, coincidentally on the exact date of the raid. I told him no, and in jocular fashion suggested that he schedule his shipment from Maurmouth instead." Brise hesitated. "Perhaps in some remote sense this might be considered an indiscretion, were I speaking with a person other than the Director of Material Procurement."

"Precisely so," said Etzwane. "In the future, please joke with no one."

Finnerack approached Etzwane the next day. "What of Brise?"

Etzwane had already considered his response. To evade or dissemble was too compromise his integrity. "Brise claims to have maintained absolute discretion. However, he made a jocular request that Aun Sharah have freight shipments ready at Maurmouth."

Finnerack made a guttural sound. "Ah! So now we know!"

"It seems so. I must consider what to do."

Finnerack raised his blond eyebrows incredulously. "What to do? Is there any question?"

"There is indeed. Assuming that, like Sajarano, Aun Sharah favours a victory of the Roguskhoi, the matter of interest to us is 'Why?' Both Sajarano and Aun Sharah are men of Shant, born and bred. What sets them apart? Lust for power or wealth? Impossible in Sajarano's case; what more could he want? Have the Palasedrans seduced them with a drug? Have they devised a telepathic method

164

of instilling obedience? Me must get to the bottom of these matters, before the same techniques are practiced on you and me. After all, why should we be immune?"

Finnerack smiled his crooked, angry smile. "The same question has often crossed my mind, especially when you are lenient with our enemies."

"I am not lenient; be assured of this," said Etzwane. "But I must be subtle."

"What of punishment?" Finnerack demanded. "Aun Sharah contrived the deaths of twelve hundred Brave Free Men! Should he escape because of subtlety?"

"His guilt is not proved. To kill Aun Sharah on suspicion, or because of rage, could do absolutely no good. We must learn his motives?"

"What then of the Brave Free Men?" stormed Finnerack. "Must they risk their lives willy-nilly? I am responsible to them, and I must protect them."

"Finnerack, you are responsible not to the Brave Free Men, but to the central authority of Shant, which is to say: me. You must not let energy and emotion overpower your reason. Let us be clear on this. If you feel that you cannot work to a long-range plan, you had best detach yourself from the government and fix upon some other occupation." Etzwane met Finnerack's flaming blue stare. "I do not claim infallibility," he continued. "In regard to Aun Sharah, I agree that he is probably guilty. It is absolutely essential that we learn the reason behind his actions."

Finnerack said, "The knowledge is not worth the life of a single man."

"How do you know this?" demanded Etzwane. "We don't know what the reason is; how can you assess it?"

"I have no time for these matters just now," grumbled Finnerack. "The Brave Free Men occupy my time."

Here was the opportunity for which Etzwane had been hoping. "I agree that you have far too much work. I'll put someone else in charge of the Intelligence System and give you help with the Brave Free Men."

Finnerack's grin became wolfish. "I don't need any help with the Brave Free Men."

Etzwane ignored him. "Meanwhile we'll watch Aun Sharah carefully and give him no scope to harm us."

Finnerack had departed. Etzwane sat thinking. Events seemed to be going favourably. The new weapons were successful; Mialambre and Dystar, each in his way, contributed to the new nation which Shant must now become. Finnerack with his passion and obstinacy posed the most immediate problem; he was not a man to be easily controlled, or even influenced. . . . Etzwane gave a bark of sardonic laughter. When, alone and fearful, he had yearned for a loyal and trustworthy henchman, the image of the placid blond boy at Angwin Junction had come to his mind. The Finnerack Etzwane had finally recruited was a man totally unsuited to Etzwane's needs; he was stubborn, wayward, cantankerous, headstrong, secretive, moody, inflexible, vengeful, narrow-minded, pessimistic, uncooperative, perhaps neither trustworthy nor loyal. Finnerack admittedly had done excellent work with the Brave Free Men and the Intelligence Agency, all of which was beside the point. Etzwane's original fear had now dissipated. No matter what his own fate, the war against the Roguskhoi had created its own momentum. New Shant was an irrevocable reality. In twenty years, for better or worse, torcs would be museum pieces and the Anome would wield a different sort of power. (Who would then be Anome? Mialambre: Octagon? Dystar? San-Sein?)

Etzwane went to look down into Corporation Plaza. Dusk was coming on. Tonight he must consider tactics in regard to Aun Sharah.

He departed his office and descended to the plaza. The folk of Garwiy had now learned of the great victory at Maurmouth; as he walked Etzwane could hear fragments of excited conversation. He was reminded of Finnerack's gloomy prognostication; conceivably Finnerack was right. The worst might be yet to come.

Etzwane went to his suite in the Roseale Hrindiana, where he planned to bathe, dine, read intelligence reports, perhaps dally a bit with Dashan of Szandales. . . . He opened the door. The suite was dim, almost dark. Unusual! Who had turned down the lights? He stepped within and touched the light-wand. Illumination failed to come. Etzwane became dizzy. The air held an odd, acid tang. He staggered to a divan, then, thinking better of relaxing, started to the door. His senses failed him. He tried to reach and grope; he felt the door latch. . . . A hand took his arm and led him sagging back into the room.

All was not as it should be, thought Etzwane. He felt peculiarly uneasy, yet fatigued and torpid, as if his sleep had been interrupted by dreams. He sat up from his couch, unaccountably weak; perhaps he had dreamt indeed: the dark, the numbness, the hand on his arm, then – voices.

Etzwane rose to his feet and went to look out across the Hrindiana gardens. The time was early morning: about the time he usually arose. He went into the bathroom, and stared in wonder at the haggard face in the

167

mirror. His beard was a dark stubble; his pupils were large and dark. He bathed, shaved himself, dressed, and descended to the garden, where he took breakfast. He found himself to be ravenously hungry and thirsty as well. . . . Strange. With his breakfast came a copy of the morning journal. He chanced to notice the date – Shristday? Yesterday had been Zaelday; today was Ettaday. . . . Shristday? Something was wrong.

He walked slowly to the Jurisdictionary. Dashan greeted him with excitement and wonder. "Where have you been? We have all been helpless with anxiety!"

"I've been away," said Etzwane. "Somewhere."

"For three days? You should have let me know," scolded Dashan.

Finnerack likewise had been gone three days, reflected Etzwane. Strange.

CHAPTER ELEVEN

In Garwiy a new feeling pervaded the air: hope and elation, mingled with melancholy for the passing of a long and placid era. Children no longer took the torc, and it was understood that after the war all deserving persons might have their torcs removed. What then of law and discipline? Who would keep the peace when the Anome lost the last of his coercive powers? For all the elation a degree of uncertainty could be felt everywhere. Etzwane brooded long hours over the situation. He was, so he feared, bequeathing to the new Anome a vexing array of problems.

Dystar came to Garwiy and presented himself to Etzwane. "To the best of my ability I have done your bidding. My task is at an end. The folk of Shant are one; events have made them one."

Etzwane realized suddenly that his indecision had been artificial. The Anome of Shant must be a man of the broadest possible scope, the most profound imagination. "Dystar," said Etzwane, "your task is done, but another awaits, which only you can fulfil."

"This I doubt," said Dystar. "What is the task?"

"You are now Anome of Shant."

"What? . . . Nonsense. I am Dystar."

Etzwane was taken aback by Dystar's displeasure. He said stiffly, "My hopes are only for Shant. Someone must be Anome; I thought to choose the best."

Dystar, now half-amused, spoke in a milder voice: "I have neither taste nor facility for such affairs. Who am I to judge the theft of a bullock or calculate the tax on candles? If I had power, my deeds would be wild and ruinous: towers among the clouds, pleasure barges a mile long to waft musicians through the isles of the Beljamar, expeditions to the Lost Kingdom of Caraz. No, Gastel Etzwane; your vision exceeds your practicality: often the case with a musician. Employ the wise Mialambre for your Anome, or better, use none at all; what advantage in an Anome when there are no torcs to explode?"

"All very well," said Etzwane in a huff, "but – reverting to the practicality which I so miserably lack – who would govern in this case? who would order? who would punish?"

Dystar had lost interest in the matter. "These are tasks for specialists, folk who have interest in such affairs.... As for myself, I must take myself away, perhaps to Shkoriy. I can play no more music; I am done."

Etzwane leaned forward in wonder. "You cannot expect me to believe this! What can be your reason?"

Dystar smiled and shrugged. "I escaped the torc; I knew the exaltation of freedom, to my great melancholy."

"Hmmf ... But do not go to Shkoriy to brood; what could be more futile? Seek out Frolitz, attach yourself to his troupe; here is cure for melancholy, I can assure you of this."

"You are right," said Dystar. "It is what I will do. I thank you for your wise advice."

For two moments the secret trembled on Etzwane's tongue, but he said only: "I wish I could join you." Certainly, on some merry night in a far tavern, while the troupe drank wine and talked at large, Fordyce or Mielke or Cune or even Frolitz would confide to Dystar his connection with Etzwane.

Dystar had gone his way. As an idle exercise Etzwane tried to contrive a theoretical government which might serve Shant as well as a wise and decisive Anome. He became interested in his construction; he refined and modified, and presently evolved what seemed a feasible disposition.

He specified two interacting organs of government. The first, a Council of Patricians, would include the directors of transportation, trade and economics, communication, law and justice, military forces, an Aesthete of Garwiy, a musician, a scientist, a historian, two persons of eminence, and two persons selected by the second council. The Council of Patricians would be self-perpetuating, selecting its own members, discharging them by a consensus of two-thirds. One of the group would be chosen First of Shant, to serve a term of three years or until voted from office by a consensus of two-thirds.

The second body, the Council of Cantons, would comprise representatives from each of the sixty-two cantons and additional delegates from the cities Garwiy, Brassei, Maschein, Oswiy, Ilwiy, and Whearn.

The Council of Cantons might propose acts and measures to the Council of Patricians and further might expel a member of the Council of Patricians by a two-thirds vote. A separate College of Justice would guarantee equity to each person of Shant. The Director of Law and Justice, sitting on the Council of Patricians, would be selected from the fellows of the College of Laws.

Etzwane called together Mialambre: Octagon, Doneis, San-Sein, Brise, and Finnerack and set forth his proposals. All agreed that the system merited at least a trial, and only Finnerack put forth serious objections. "You overlook one matter: at large and living in Shant are the magnates who won their ease through the pain of others. Should not the concept of indemnification be codified into the new system?"

"This is more properly a matter of adjudication," said Etzwane.

Finnerack warmed to his subject. "Further, why should some toil for a mouthful of bread while long-fingered sybarites partake of Forty-Five Dishes? The good things should be divided; we should start the new system on a basis of equality."

Mialambre responded: "Your sentiments are generous and do you credit. All I can say it that such drastic redistributions have previously been attempted, always to result in chaos and cruel tyranny of one sort or another. This is the lesson of history, which we must now heed."

Finnerack offered no further opinions.

Seven companies of Brave Free Men, augmented by the now enthusiastic militia, attacked the Roguskhoi on four broad fronts. The Roguskhoi, adapting to their new vulnerability, moved by night, sheltered in forests and wildernesses, attacked by surprise, seeking always women, sometimes at vast risk to themselves. Grudgingly they retreated from the coast, back through cantons Marestiy and Faible.

Etzwane received a report from Doneis, the Director of Technical Achievement. "The Roguskhoi imps have been studied at length. They prove to be creatures of the most peculiar sort, and it is hard to understand their human semblance; nevertheless they require a human woman as hostess for their spawn. In what conceivable environment could they have so evolved?"

"In Palasedra, so it has been suggested."

"This is possible; Palasedrans have long been evolving a warrior sort. Certain Caraz mariners claim to have seen the creatures. It is a great puzzle."

"Have you learned how the Roguskhoi identify women?"

"There was no problem here. One of the female essences lures them. They are drawn as sure as an ahulph strikes carrion; they will detect the most evanescent whiff and strive through any obstacle to sate themselves."

The Brave Free Men now numbered over five thousand. Finnerack had become more remote and single-minded than ever; rancour seemed to burn inside him like fire in a stove. Etzwane's uneasiness grew in proportion. To reduce the scope of Finnerack's authority, Etzwane fragmented the leadership into five phases. Black Finnerack became Captain of Strategy; San-Sein was Captain of Field Operations; additionally there were Captains of Logistics, Recruitment and Training, and Weaponry.

Finnerack protested the new situation in a cold fury. "Always you make things more cumbersome! In the place of one Anome you give us a hundred politicians; for one responsible and efficient commander you substitute a committee of five. Is this sensible? I wonder at your motives!"

"They are simple," said Etzwane. "An Anome can no longer control Shant; a hundred men are needed. The war, the armies of Shant, their strategy, tactics, and goals are likewise too large for the control of a single man."

Finnerack removed his black hat and threw it into a corner. "You underestimate me."

"This, I assure you, is not the case," said Etzwane.

The two examined each other for a moment without friendliness. Etzwane said, "Sit down a moment; I want to ask you something."

Finnerack went to a divan, leaned back, thrust his black boots out across the Burazhesq rug. "What is your question?"

"A short time ago you disappeared for three days. When you returned you gave no account of your whereabouts. What happened to you during this time?"

Finnerack gave a sour grunt. "It is unimportant."

"I think not," said Etzwane. "A short time ago I went to my suite and was drugged by some sort of gas, or so I suppose. I awoke three days later, without any knowledge of what had transpired. Is this what happened to you?"

"More or less," Finnerack brought the words forth reluctantly.

"Have you noticed any consequences of this event? Do you feel yourself different in any way?"

Finnerack again paused before replying. "Of course there are no differences. Do you feel differences?"

"No. None whatever."

Finnerack had departed; Etzwane still lacked insight into the workings of Finnerack's mind. Finnerack had no obvious weaknesses: no yearning for ease, wealth, drink, fair women, soft living. Etzwane could not say as much for himself, though recognizing the dangers of self-indulgence he tried to live in relative austerity. Dashan of Szandales, either by her initiative or his own – Etzwane had never felt certain of the matter – had become his mistress. The situation pleased Etzwane because of its convenience. In due course, when once again he became a musician, the situation no doubt would alter.

San-Sein, the Captain of Field Operations, one morning came into Etzwane's office with a roll of charts. "We are presented an opportunity of great promise," he stated. "The Roguskhoi have broken; they retreat towards the Hwan. One horde moves south through Ascalon and Seamus, another in Ferriy has pulled back into Bastern, and this column from Cansume has entered South Marestiy and marches towards Bundoran. Do you see where they tend?"

"If they plan to return into the Wildlands, they more than likely will pass up Mirk Valley."

"Exactly. Now here is my plan, which I have already discussed and cleared with Finnerack. Suppose that we harry the column close on the rear, enough to keep them curious, but that here at Mirk Defile we prepare an ambush."

"All very well," said Etzwane, "but how do you bring troops to Mirk Defile?"

"Notice the balloon-way and the prevailing winds. If we loaded forty balloons at Oswiy and let them fly free they would reach Mirk Defile in six hours. The winch-tender need only put down to discharge troops, then continue south to the Great Ridge Route."

Etzwane considered. "The idea sounds appealing. But

175

what of the winds? I was born in Bashon and as I recall they blow up the Mirk as often as down. Have you spoken to the meteorologists?"

"Not yet. Here are the wind arrows on the chart."

"The project is far too chancy. Suppose we run into a calm? They often occur about this time. We'd have forty balloonloads of men lost deep in the Wildlands. Rather than balloons we need gliders." Etzwane suddenly remembered the builders of Canton Whearn. He reflected a moment, then bent over the map. "Mirk Defile is the obvious route. Suppose the Roguskhoi learned of the ambush? They might very well turn aside at Bashon and head west, past Kozan, before turning south into the Wildlands. We can put troops into Kozan without difficulty; the balloonway passes only twenty miles west. Here on Kozan Bluffs is where we must set up our ambush."

"But how do we apprise the Roguskhoi of the Mirk ambush, so that they will turn aside?"

"Leave that to me. I know a subtle method. If it succeeds, well and good. If it fails, we are no worse off than before. Your instructions are these: confide to no one that the Mirk Valley ambush is non-operative. The secret must lie between you and me alone. Ready your troops at Oswiy; load the balloons but, rather than allowing them to drift free, send them south along the balloon-way into Seamus. Disembark, march to Kozan Bluffs, and establish your ambush."

San-Sein was gone. The plot had been set into motion. Once again Brise would be the instrument of news leakage to Aun Sharah.

Etzwane went to his telephone and called the Intelligence Agency radio operator. "Make contact with Pelmonte in Canton Whearn. Request that the Superinten-

176

dent be brought to the microphone, and thereupon notify me."

An hour later Etzwane heard the voice of the Superintendent of Whearn. Etzwane said, "Do you remember when Gastel Etzwane, the Anome's assistant, passed through Whearn several months ago?"

"I do indeed."

"At such time I recommended that you build gliders. What progress have you made in this direction?"

"We have done your bidding. We have built gliders to the best design. With a dozen complete, and with no word from you, we have somewhat slowed the pace of our construction."

"Proceed once again at full haste. I will send men to Whearn to take delivery."

"Do you plan to send flyers?"

"We have none to send."

"Then they must be trained. Select a contingent of your best, send them to Pelmonte. In due course they will fly the gliders wherever you wish."

"This is what shall be done. Thanks to men like yourself the Roguskhoi are in retreat. We have come a long way these last few months."

CHAPTER TWELVE

Brise spoke to Etzwane. "I have followed your instructions. Aun Sharah knows of the Mirk ambush. It is a job for which I do not consider myself fitted."

"Nor more do I. But the job must be done. Now we will wait for eventualities."

Reports came hourly to Etzwane. A Roguskhoi column formed of four raiding parties, representing the total force which had subdued northeast Shant, marched south down the Mirk Valley, accompanied by an unknown number of captive women. Brave Free Men mounted on pacers harried the Roguskhoi flanks and rearguard, and themselves suffered casualties as a result of Roguskhoi counter manoeuvres; the route of the column was marked by a line of corpses.

The horde approached Bashon, where the temple, deserted and forlorn, had already entered the first stages of decay.

At Rhododendron Way the column paused. Six chieftains, conspicuous for bibs and chain mail hanging over their chests, conferred and peered down Mirk Valley towards the Hwan. There was, however, no indecision; they swung west along Rhododendron Way, passing under the great, dark trees. Hearing the news, Etzwane remembered an urchin named Mur playing in the white dust under these same trees. At the end of Rhododendron Way, with open country before them, the chieftains paused once again to confer. An order was passed down the column; a score of warriors stepped off into the foliage beside the Way. The threat of their scimitars effectually prevented any close pursuit by the cavalry, which must now retreat and circle either north or south of the Way.

The Roguskhoi left the main road and slanted south into the Hwan foothills. Above them bulked Kozan Bluffs, a knob of grey limestone pocked by ancient caves and tunnels.

The Roguskhoi approached the bluff. In the west appeared a company of Brave Free Men; from the east came the cavalry which had harried the rear. The Roguskhoi jogged down towards the Hwan, passing close under Kozan Bluff. From the holes and crannies came sudden white streaks of gunfire. From the east the Brave Free Men cavalry approached; and likewise from the west.

placards of purple, green, pale blue, and white announced the new government of Shant:

> The Brave Free Men have liberated out country. For this we rejoice and celebrate the unity of Shant. The Anome has graciously given way to an open and responsive government, consisting of a Purple House of Patricians and a Green House of the Cantons. Already three manifestos have been issued:
>
> There are to be no more torcs.
> The indenture programme is to be highly modified.
> Religious systems may commit no further crimes.

The Purple Patricians include the following:

Listed were the directors and their functions. Gastel Etzwane, a director-at-large, was declared Executive Director. The second director-at-large was Jerd Finnerack. San-Sein was Director of Military Affairs.

Aun Sharah occupied the top floor of an ancient blue and white glass structure behind Corporation Plaza, almost under the Ushkadel. His office was very large, almost eccentrically bare of furnishing. The high north wall consisted entirely of clear glass panes. The worktable was at the centre of the room; Aun Sharah sat looking north through the great expanse of glass. When Etzwane and Finnerack entered the room, he nodded courteously and rose to his feet. For five seconds a silence held; the three stood each in his attitude in the great bare room, fateful as players on a stage.

Etzwane spoke formally, "Aun Sharah, we are forced to the conviction that you are working adversely to the interests of Shant."

Aun Sharah smiled as if Etzwane had paid him a compliment. "It is hard to please everybody."

Finnerack took a slow step forward, then drew back and said nothing.

Etzwane, somewhat nonplussed by Aun Sharah's agreeable demeanour, spoke on. "The fact of your actions is established. Still, we are puzzled as to your motives. In fostering the cause of the Roguskhoi, how do you gain, how do you serve yourself?"

Aun Sharah, still smiling – peculiarly, so Etzwane thought – asked: "Has the fact been demonstrated?"

"Abundantly. Your conduct has been under scrutiny for several months. You prompted Shirge Hillen of Camp Three to kill me; you put spies on my movements. As Director of Material Procurement you have in several instances substantially lessened the war effort by diverting labour into non-essential projects. At Thran in Green Stone your ambush of Brave Free Men failed, by luck alone. In the engagement at Kozan Bluff we have achieved decisive proof. You were informed that Mirk Defile was to be guarded, whereupon the Roguskhoi veered aside and were destroyed. The reality of your guilt is established. Your motives are a cause for perplexity."

The three again stood silently in the centre of the vast, bleak room.

"Please sit down," said Aun Sharah gently. "You have pelted me with such a barrage of nonsense that my mind is confused and my knees are weak." Etzwane and Finnerack remained standing; Aun Sharah sat down and took up stylus and paper. "Please repeat your bill of charges, if you will."

Etzwane did so, and Aun Sharah made a list. "Five items: all wind and no susbstance. Many men have been destroyed for as little."

Etzwane began to feel perplexed. "You deny the charges then?"

Aun Sharah smiled his curious smile. "Let me ask rather, can you prove any of the charges?"

"We can," said Finnerack.

"Very well," said Aun Sharah. "We will consider the items one at a time – but let us call in the jurist Mialambre: Octagon to weigh the evidence, and Director of Transportation Brise as well."

"I see no objection to this," said Etzwane. "Let us go to my office."

Back in his old office Aun Sharah waved the others to seats, as if they were underlings he had summoned to conference. He addressed Mialambre: "Not half an hour ago Gastel Etzwane and Black Finnerack entered my office to deliver a set of five charges, so preposterous that I suspect their sanity. The charges are these:" Aun Sharah read off his list.

"The first accusation, that I notified Shirge Hillen of Etzwane's coming is no more than an unfounded suspicion, the more vicious in that Etzwane has made no attempt to find an alternative solution. I suggested that he investigate the balloon-way offices; this he neglected to do. I made a few quiet inquiries; in twenty minutes I learned that a certain Parway Harth had in fact sent out an intemperate and somewhat ambiguous message which Shirge Hillen might well have understood as an order to kill Gastel Etzwane. I can prove this three different ways; through Parway Harth, through a subordinate who took the message to the balloon-way radio, and through the files in the balloon-way radio office.

"Item Two: the charge that I put spies upon Gastel Etzwane. The reference is to a surveillance performed by one of my trackers: an act of casual interest. I do not deny this charge; I claim that it is too trivial to be significant of anything whatever.

"Item Three: as Director of Material Procurement I have in several instances diminished the war effort. In hundreds of instances I have augmented the war effort. I complained to Gastel Etzwane that my abilities did not lie in this direction; he stubbornly ignored my statement.

If the war effort suffered, the fault is his alone. I did my best.

"Items Four and Five: I arranged a Roguskhoi ambush at Thran and I attempted to betray an ambush of our own in Mirk Valley. A few days ago I stepped into the office of Director Brise. In a most peculiar and embarrassed manner he contrived an elephantine hint as to an ambush in Mirk Valley. I am a suspicious man, skilled at intrigue. I detected a plot. I declared as much to Brise; I further insisted that he leave me alone not for an instant, day or night; he must absolutely assure himself that I had transmitted no information. I convinced him that such was his duty to Shant, that if any ambush were in fact betrayed we must learn the true culprit. To do this we must be able to demonstrate my innocence beyond argument. He is a reasonable and honourable man; he agreed to my analysis of the situation. I ask you now, Brise: did I, during the applicable period, inform anyone at any time of anything whatsoever?"

"You did not," said Brise shortly. "You sat in my office, in my company and that of my trusted associates, for two days. You communicated with no one, you betrayed no ambush."

"We received news of the battle at Kozan," Aun Sharah went on. "Brise now confessed to me that he considered himself to blame for the fact that suspicion had fallen upon me. He reported his conversation with Gastel Etzwane.

"I understand now that I am linked to the ambush at Thran by one question and one answer. I required that Brise send bottoms to Oswiy; he said no, I must send my goods to Maurmouth. On this basis my guilt in regard to the Thran ambush is assumed. The concept is far fetched

183

but remotely possible, except for a secondary fact which once again Gastel Etzwane has not noticed. This question and this answer, in a thousand variations, has become a joke between Brise and myself: repartee as we coordinate our functions. I ask him for transport at one place, he says impossible, find freight at another. Brise, is this correct?"

"It is correct," said Brise in an uncomfortable voice. "The question and the answer might be repeated five times a day. Aun Sharah could have understood nothing of significance in the remarks regarding Oswiy and Thran. I reported them to Gastel Etzwane because he required my every word; I neglected to put them into context."

Aun Sharah asked Etzwane: "Do you have any other charges?"

Etzwane gave a sick laugh. "None. I am clearly unfit to make a rational judgment on anyone or anything. I apologize to you and will make amends as best I can. I must seriously consider resigning from the Purple House."

Mialambre: Octagon spoke in a gruff voice: "Come now, the matter need go no farther; this is no time for extravagant acts."

"Except in this single regard," said Aun Sharah. "You spoke of amends. If you are serious, return me to my own work; give me back my Discriminators."

"So far as I am concerned," said Etzwane, "they are yours, any that are left. Finnerack has turned the place inside out."

The Roguskhoi had been driven back into the Wildlands, and for a period the war dwindled to a halt. Finnerack presented his estimate of the situation to Etzwane. "They are as if in an impregnable fortress. Our radius of

184

penetration is twenty miles; beyond this line the Rogusk-hoi breed, re-arm, re-group, and presumably re-cast their strategies."

Etzwane mused. "We have captured thousands of scimitars; they are made of an alloy unknown in Shant. What is the source of supply? Do they operate foundries deep in the Hwan? A great mystery."

Finnerack gave an indifferent nod. "Our strategy now is self-evident. We must organize our total manpower and gradually occupy the Hwan. It is a toilsome and complicated task, but is there any other method?"

"Probably not," said Etzwane.

"Then back to Palasedra with the brutes! And let the Palasedrans interfere at their peril!"

"Presuming that the Palasedrans are responsible, which is not yet proved."

Finnerack stared in astonishment. "Who else but the Palasedrans?"

"Who else but Aun Sharah? I have learned my lesson."

CHAPTER THIRTEEN

Summer brought a lull to the war, which extended into the long mild autumn. Shant repaired its damage, mourned its dead men and kidnapped women, augmented its armed might. The Brave Free Men, expanding in numbers and organization, separated into regional divisions, with the cantonal militia serving functions of support and supply. Weapons poured from the Shranke assemblies; the Roguskhoi scimitars, melted and moulded, became ballast.

Gliders flew forth from Whearn: double-winged craft, light as moths. A special corps of the Brave Free Men became the Flyers of Shant. Their training at first was makeshift and merciless; those who survived instructed the others. By sheer necessity the Flyers became a skilled and cohesive force, and as natural consequence began to make prideful demonstration of reckless daring and élan.

To arm the gliders, the technists produced a ferocious new weapon, a simplified, non-ballasted version of the halcoid gun. The projectile was composite: halcoid joined to a metal, the firing tube was open at each end. When fired, the halcoid struck forward, the metal was ejected aft; in effect the weapon acted in both directions, eliminating recoil and the need for ballast. When fired from a glider, the ejected missile usually spent itself harmlessly in the air; on the ground the guns were intolerably dangerous.

Before sending gliders out against the Roguskhoi, Finnerack drilled the Flyers in battle tactics, the dropping of bombs with accuracy, and safety techniques with respect to the halcoid gun.

From the first Finnerack had been fascinated with the gliders; he learned to fly, and presently, not altogether to Etzwane's surprise, he relinquished his command over the Brave Free Men in order to assume control of the Flyers.

In the middle of autumn the ground armies began to move up into the Hwan, pushing west from Cansume, Haghead, and Lor-Asphen, retaking cantons Surrume and Shkoriy. A second force moved south through Bastern, Seamus, and Bundoran, into the Wildlands itself. Other companies worked east and south, from Shade and Sable, penetrating the Mount Misk region, and here the Roguskhoi put up fierce resistance. Theirs was now a lost cause. Trained ahulphs spied out their concentrations, which then were bombed or subjected to halcoid fire from guns mounted in clusters of six.

On other occasions the Roguskhoi were baited into ambush by lures of "female essence," to which they were intensely responsive. Another time, gliders sprayed a Roguskhoi camp with a solution of "female essence" with horrid effect. The Roguskhoi, confused by the contradictory stimuli of nose and eye, seemed to become insanely cantankerous; in short order they were cuffing each other and then exchanging bludgeon blows, until almost all were dead; at once gliders set out across all the Wildlands laden not with dexax but with canisters of "female essence."

Ahulphs, somewhat belatedly set out to spy, reported the course of the Roguskhoi supply route. It led from the Great Salt Bog into the swamps of Canton Shker, then proceeded north under a dense forest of raintree and parasol daraba, up through the Moaning Mountains and into the Hwan.

The military command dispatched a force to cut the line at the forest edge. Finnerack wanted to react more vehemently. "Is this not evidence? The Palasedrans are responsible. The Salt Bog is no barrier; why should they be spared a taste of their own medicine?"

The command captains frowned down at their charts, lacking argument against convictions so emphatic. Finnerack, somewhat chastened after the Aun Sharah fiasco, had been reanimated by his new role as Flyer. He now wore a Flyer uniform of fine black cloth, cut to something more than ordinary flair. Here, thought Etzwane, with the Flyers of Shant, was Finnerack's natural function: he had never before seemed so zestful and energetic. The power and freedom of flight had exalted him; he walked the world like a man apart, superior in basic fibre to the groundlings, who would never know the terrible joys of sweeping silently across the hills, rising and falling, circling, veering, then swooping like a hawk to blast apart a marching column.... Etzwane had long lost all fear of Finnerack's turning the Brave Free Men against the government. Too many safeguards had been set up; in retrospect Etzwane saw that he might have been over-cautious. Finnerack showed no interest in the sources of power;

he seemed satisfied to crush his enemies. For Finnerack, Etzwane thought, a world without enemies would be a very dull place. He now answered Finnerack in his most reasonable voice: "We don't want to punish the Palasedrans for at least three reasons. First, we're not yet finished with the Roguskhoi. Second, Palasedran responsibility is not certain. Third, it would be a poor policy to embroil ourselves needlessly in a war with the Palasedrans. They are a fierce people who give back twice as good as they take, as Shant has learned to its sorrow. Suppose the Roguskhoi are an oversight, a mistake? Or the work of a dissident group? We can't plunge Shant into a war so recklessly. After all, what do we know of Palasedra? Nothing. The place is a closed book to us."

"We know enough," said Finnerack. "They have bred an array of weird soldier-beasts, this we learn from Caraz mariners. We find the Roguskhoi trail leading into the Salt Bog towards Palasedra. These are facts."

"True. But they are not all the facts. We need more knowledge. I will send an envoy to Chemaoue."

Finnerack gave a bitter laugh and swung half about in his chair, the helmet of the Flyers askew on his blond curls.

Etzwane said: "We need be neither weak nor truculent; we are not forced to make such a choice. We will drive the Roguskhoi from our lands, and meanwhile we must try to learn the Palasedran intentions. Only a fool acts before thinking, as I have learned."

Finnerack turned to look at Etzwane; the blue eyes showed a narrow glitter, like sunlight reflecting from a far ledge of ice. Then he shrugged and sat back in his seat, a man at peace with himself.

The Roguskhoi were in retreat. The Brave Free Men thrusting into the Hwan from Shade, Sable, Seamus, and Bastern suddenly encountered no resistance whatever. Glider patrols and free balloon reconnaissance told the same story: the Roguskhoi were streaming south in dozens of columns. For the most part they moved by night, taking what shelter they could during the day. Gliders harassed them from overhead, spitting halcoid, dropping bombs of dexax. "Female essence" had lost its initial effect; the Roguskhoi, while perturbed and agitated, no longer indulged in suicidal paroxysms.

The Flyers were at the pinnacle of their glory. The blue and white uniforms aroused a delirium of adulation; nothing was too good for a Flyer of Shant.

Finnerack likewise had reached his zenith. Watching him as he dealt with business of the Flyers, Etzwane found it hard to recall the pleasant-faced boy he had known at Angwin Junction. For all practical purposes, the boy had died at Camp Three.... What of the small, dark, pinch-faced boy who had escaped Angwin Junction? Looking in the carbon-fume mirror, Etzwane saw a face hollow-cheeked and sallow, with a mouth straight and still.... He had known a rich life indeed, thought Etzwane. If Finnerack were now at the crest of his career, Etzwane considered his work done. He longed to detach himself – to become what? A wandering musician once more? Shant seemed suddenly too small, too limited. Palasedra was a hostile land; Caraz a vast mystery. The name Ifness came into Etzwane's mind. He thought of the planet Earth.

The Roguskhoi, commanded by their roaring chieftains, loped down from the Wildlands, through Canton Shker, and into the Great Salt Bog. The Brave Free Men, attacking on the flanks, took a terrible toll, as did the Flyers, veering, swooping, projecting streaks of incandescent air.

The columns dwindled to a trickle, then ended. The Brave Free Men roamed the length and breadth of the Hwan, finding an occasional sickly imp or bands of starving women, but no more Roguskhoi.

Shant was free of its invaders. The Roguskhoi had retired into the Great Salt Bog, a place of black ooze, rust-coloured ponds, occasional islands overgrown with coral trees, other islands of sand rising stark and bare, pale green reeds, snakegrass, black limberleaf.

In the Salt Bog the Roguskhoi seemed secure and easy and wallowed effortlessly through the ooze. The Brave Free Men pursued until the ground grew soft, then reluctantly drew back. The Flyers knew no such limits. The black morasses, the knolls of bright white sand, the coral-tree forests, the winds thrusting in from both the Blue and Purple Oceans created draughts and shafts of rising and falling air; sunlight shimmered down between tall thunderheads; the gliders soared and swooped at will, no longer pursuing, now wreaking vengeance.

Deeper and deeper into the Great Salt Bog moved the Roguskhoi, harried by the merciless gliders. Etzwane felt impelled to caution Finnerack: "Whatever else, do not enter alien territory! Hector the Roguskhoi as you like, back and forth across the Great Salt Bog, but under no circumstances provoke the Palasedrans!"

Finnerack showed his small, hard grin. "The boundaries are where? In the centre of the Bog? Show me where the exact line lies."

"So far as I know there is no precise boundary. The

Salt Bog is like a sea. If you verged too close against the southern shore of the Bog, the Palasedrans would claim encroachment."

"Bog is bog," said Finnerack. "I understand the Palasedran's distress, but I give them no compassion."

"This is beside the point," said Etzwane patiently. "Your orders are: do not operate your gliders within sight of Palasedra."

Finnerack stood bristling in front of Etzwane, who for the first time felt the uncloaked thrust of Finnerack's hatred. Etzwane was affected by a sensation of physical disgust. Finnerack was a good hater. When Etzwane had first identified himself, Finnerack had admitted hate for the boy who had caused him woe, but had not the balance been righted? Etzwane drew a slow, deep breath. Conditions were as they were.

Finnerack had spoken, in a low, dangerous voice: "Do you still give me orders, Gastel Etzwane?"

"I do, by authority of the Purple House. Do you serve Shant, or the gratification of your personal passions?"

Finnerack stared at Etzwane ten seconds, then swung away and departed.

The envoy returned from his mission to Chemaoue, with no satisfactory news. "I could make no direct contact with the Eagle-Dukes. They are proud and remote. I cannot fathom their purposes. I received a message to the effect that they could not deal with slaves; if we wanted transactions, we must send down the Anome. I replied that Shant no longer was under the Anome's rule, that I was an emissary of the Purple and Green, but they seemed not to heed."

Etzwane conferred in private with Aun Sharah, who once more occupied his old office overlooking Corporation Plaza.

"I have assiduously studied both sets of circumstances," said Aun Sharah. "In regard to the two ambushes the essential facts are clear. Four persons were informed as to the Thran operation: yourself, San-Sein, Finnerack, and Brise. You and San-Sein knew of the Kozan Bluff ambush, which succeeded; you two are eliminated. Brise most certainly have deduced that the Mirk Valey ambush was bogus; he might easily have presumed the Kozan Bluff ambush. He too can be eliminated in the Mirk Valley ambush. Accordingly we must regard Finnerack as the traitor."

Etzwane was silent a moment. Then he said, "I have thought along these same lines. The logic is sound; the conclusion is absurd. How can the most zealous warrior of Shant be a traitor?"

"I don't know," said Aun Sharah. "I returned to this office, I altered arrangements to suit myself, as you see. In the process I discovered a whole array of eavesdrop devices. I took the liberty of inspecting your suite at the Hrindiana, where I found another such set. Finnerack of course had easy opportunity to arrange these devices."

"Incredible," muttered Etzwane. "Have you located the terminus of the system?"

"They feed into a radio transmitter, which broadcasts continuously at a low level."

"The devices, the radio — they are Shant manufacture?"

"They are standard Discriminator adjuncts."

"Hmmf ... For the present we'll wait and watch. I don't care to make any more premature accusations."

Aun Sharah smiled thoughtfully. "Now as to the second investigation: I learned very little. Finnerack simply dropped from sight for three days. Two men of Canton Parthe occupied the suite next to Finnerack. They departed a day or so after Finnerack's 'return.' I took detailed descriptions and I feel that they were not Parthans, whatever the colour of their torcs: they hung up no door fetish and frequently wore blue.

"I naturally made inquiry at the Roseale Hrindiana. Two similar men occupied the suite directly above yours prior to your experience. They then departed without notifying the Hrindiana officials."

"I am baffled," said Etzwane. "I also am greatly afraid. ... I asked Finnerack if he felt differently; he said no. I feel no differently either."

Aun Sharah regarded Etzwane curiously, then made one of his delicate gestures. "I can tell you no more. Naturally I am searching for the Parthans, and Finnerack is being kept under unobtrusive observation. Something suggestive may turn up."

The Flyers of Shant pressed the Roguskhoi ever deeper into the bog, giving no respite; the air above the great morass stunk of carrion. The Roguskhoi moved always southward – towards a destination? to put all distance between themselves and the Flyers of Shant? No one could say, but presently the northern half of the Salt Bog was as empty of Roguskhoi as Shant itself.

In the gallant colours of victory, the journals of Garwiy published a proclamation of the Purple and Green:

The war must now be considered at an end, although the Flyers continue to wreak retribution for the countless Roguskhoi atrocities. It is impossible to feel pity for the brutes.

However, we must now terminate our campaign. The glorious feats of the Brave Free Men and the Flyers of Shant will live forever in the history of the race. These noble men must now devote their energies to the regeneration of Shant.

THE WAR IS AT AN END

Finnerack was late to the meeting of the Purple House. Entering the chamber, he marched with slow steps to his place at the marble table.

Etzwane was speaking. "Our great struggle is done, and I feel that my responsibility is ended. This being the case —"

Finnerack interrupted him. "One moment, so that you may not be resigning under a misapprehension. I have just now received news from Shker. The Flyers of Shant, operating in the southern area of the Great Salt Bog, this morning encountered a dense column of Roguskhoi making at speed for the Palasedran shore. We attacked and approached Palasedra. Our manoeuvres were under careful surveillance, and it may be that the Roguskhoi movements were intended to draw us into a condition of technical incursion." Finnerack paused. "This was the event. Our gliders were intercepted by black Palasedran gliders, flown with great skill. In the first engagement they destroyed four gliders of Shant, losing none. In the second engagement we altered our tactics and shot down two enemy gliders, while losing two more of our own. I have received no further reports."

Mialambre broke the silence. "But you were instructed to avoid a close approach to Palasedra."

"Our basic purpose," said Finnerack, "is to destroy the enemy. His whereabouts is immaterial."

"You may think so. I do not. Must we fight a new Palasedran war because of your intractability?"

"We have already been fighting a Palasedran war," said Finnerack. "The Roguskhoi were not generated out of nothingness."

"This is your opinion! Who gave you the right to act for all Shant?"

"A person does what his inner soul directs." Finnerack jerked his head towards Etzwane. "Who gave him the right to take to himself the authority of the Anome? He had no more right than I."

"The difference is real," retorted Mialambre. "A man sees a house on fire. He rouses the inhabitants and extinguishes the blaze. Another, in order to punish the arsonist, fires a village. One man is a hero, the other is a maniac."

San-Sein said: "Black Finnerack, your courage is beyond all question. Unfortunately, your zeal is excessive. Recklessness destroys our freedom of action. Convey these orders instantly to the Flyers of Shant: return to the home territory! Do not again fare forth into the Great Salt Bog until so commanded!"

Finnerack moved his helmet, tossed it upon the marble. "I cannot give these orders. They are not realistic. When the Flyers of Shant are attacked, they fight back with unyielding ferocity."

"Must we send Brave Free Men to control our own Flyers?" roared San-Sein, suddenly in a fury. "If they fly forth again, we will take their gliders and rip off their uniforms! We, the Purple and Green of Shant, are in authority!"

Into the chamber burst a steward! "From the city Chemaoue in Palasedra comes a strong radio message: the Chancellor demands the voice and ear of the Anome."

The entire Council of Patricians listened to the words of the Palasedran Chancellor, spoken in a language of odd accents and altered sound quality. "I am Chancellor to the Hundred Sovereigns. I will speak to the Anome of Shant."

Etzwane spoke. "The rule of the Anome is ended. You now address the Council of Patricians; say what you will."

"I ask you then: why do you attack us after two thousand years of peace? Have not four wars and four defeats taught you to beware?"

"The attacks were directed against the Roguskhoi. We drive them back whence they came."

The atmosphere crackled softly while the Chancellor collected his thoughts. He said, "They are nothing of ours. You have driven them from the Bog into Palasedra; is this not an offensive act? You have sent your gliders into our lands; is this not an intrusion?"

"Not if, as we are convinced, you sent the Roguskhoi against us in the first place."

"We worked no such acts. Do you believe this? Send your envoys to Palasedra; you shall see for yourself. This is our generous offer. You have acted with irresponsibility. If you choose not to learn the truth, we will consider you spitefully stupid and men will die."

"We are neither spiteful nor stupid," Etzwane returned. "It is only sensible that we discuss and adjust our differences; we welcome the opportunity to do so, especially if you can demonstrate your non-involvement in our troubles."

"Send your envoys," said the Chancellor. "Fly them by a single glider to the port Kaoime; they will come to no harm, and there our escort will meet them, with proper demeanour."

CHAPTER FOURTEEN

Palasedra hung below Shant like a gnarled, three-fingered hand, with the Great Salt Bog for a wrist. The mountains of Palasedra formed the bones of the Palasedran hand. They rose in naked juts, and many held aloft the lonely castles of the Eagle-Dukes. The forests of Palasedra tumbled down the seaward valleys. Giant loutranos with straight black trunks supported disproportionately small parasols of dough-coloured pulp. Around their shanks surged a dark green froth of similax and wax-pod, which in turn towered above arbours of gohovany, argove, jajuy. The towns of Palasedra guarded the valley sea mouths. Tall stone houses with high-pitched roofs stood cramped together, one growing from the next like crystals in a rock. Palasedra! a strange, grim land, where every man reckoned himself noble and acknowledged only the authority of an "honour" which everyone recognized but no one enforced; where no door was locked, where no window was shuttered; where each man's brain was a citadel as quiet as the castle of an Eagle-Duke.

At Kaoime the glider from Shant slid to a landing on the narrow beach. Four men climbed down from the saddles within the truss. The first was the flyer, the remaining three were Etzwane, Mialambre, and Finnerack, who had agreed to visit Palasedra only after his courage, judgment, and quality of intelligence had been mocked and challenged – whereupon Finnerack declared his willingness to explore the far side of Caraz if need be.

The stern houses of Kaoime looked down from the back of the beach. Three tall men wearing fitted black gowns and high-crowned black hats came forward. Their movements were stately and mannered.

These were the first Palasedras Etzwane had seen and he examined them with interest. They exemplified a race somewhat different from his own. Their skin, pallid as parchment, showed a faint arsenical tarnish to glancing light. Their faces were long, thin, and convex, the forehead and chin receding, the nose a prow. One spoke in a muffled guttural voice, forming his words somewhere behind his palate. For this reason, and because he used a strange, oddly accented dialect, his speech was almost incomprehensible. "You are the envoys from Shant?"

"We are."

"You wear no torcs; you have for a fact thrown off the yoke of your tyrant?"

Mialambre started to make a didactic qualification; Etzwane said, "We have altered our style of government; this is a fact."

"In that case, I greet you in my official capacity. We fly at once to Chemaoue. With me then, to the sky-lift."

They mounted to a platform of woven withe. With a surge and a sway an endless cable took them aloft: up under the argoves, through a hole in the dark green mat and into the airy aisles between the loutranos, up past the dough-coloured parasols into the lavender light of the three suns. A platform stood on spider-leg stilts at the lip of a cliff; here they disembarked. A glider awaited them: an intricate device of struts, cords, vanes, with a cabin of withe and film hanging under bat-wing sails.

The one Palasedran and the three men of Shant entered the cabin. Far across the plateau a group of enormous men, indistinctly seen, thrust a wicker basket full of stones over the precipice. A cable accelerated the glider; smoothly it climbed into the sky and was launched out into the empty spaces.

The Palasedran showed no disposition for conversation. Etzwane presently asked, "You know why we are here?"

The Palasedran said, "I read no exact knowledge. Your ideas find no correspondence with mine."

"Ah," said Mialambre, "you were sent to read our minds."

"I was sent to convey you politely to Chemaoue."

"Who is Chancellor? One of the Eagle-Dukes?"

"No, we are now five castes rather than four. The Eagle-Dukes concern themselves with honour."

"We are ignorant of Palasedra and its customs," said Etzwane. "If the Chancellor is not an Eagle-Duke, how does he rule them?"

"The Chancellor rules no one. He acts only for himself."

"But he speaks for Palasedra?"

"Why not? Someone must do so."

"What if he commits you to an unpopular course of action?"

"He knows what is expected of him. It is the way we conduct ourselves, doing what is expected of us. If we fail, our sponsors bear the brunt. Is this not right?" He touched the band of his hat, which bore a dozen heraldic badges. "These folk have sponsored me. They gave me their trust. Two are Eagle-Dukes. . . . Behold yonder, the castle of Duke Ain Palaeio."

The castle occupied a saddle between two crags: a mouldering structure almost invisible against the surrounding stone. To either side stood a handful of black cypresses. Grey-green stoneflower grew in festoons down the foundation walls. . . . The castle fell behind and was lost to view.

Up columns of wind, down slopes of air floated the black glider, sliding ever southward. The mountains became lower; the loutranos disappeared; the similax and argove gave way to hangman tree, dark oak, occasional groves of cypress.

The afternoon waned; the winds and draughts became less definite. As the sun rolled behind the western mountains, the glider slid softly down towards a distant leaden shine of water, and presently landed in the dusk beside the town of Chemaoue.

A vehicle of pale varnished wood on four tall wheels stood waiting. The draught animals were naked men, bulky of leg and chest, seven feet tall, with skins of a peculiar ruddy ochre. The small neat heads lacked hair; the blunt features showed no expression. Finnerack, who had spoken little during the journey – if anything he seemed uneasy and looked frequently, almost with longing, back the way they had come – now turned Etzwane a sardonic glance, as if claiming vindication for his theories.

Mialambre demanded of the Palasedran: "These creatures are the work of your man-makers?"

"They are, though the process is not quite as you assume it to be."

"I make no assumptions; I am a jurist."

"Are never jurists irrational? Especially the jurists of Shant?"

"Why the jurists of Shant, specifically?"

"Your land is rich; you can afford irrationality."

"Not so!" declared Mialambre. "By saying this, you make all your words suspect."

"A matter of no consequence."

The carriage trundled through the dusk. Watching the heaving orange backs, Etzwane asked: "The man-makers continue to do their work in Palasedra?"

'We are imperfect.'

"What of these toiling creatures? Do they become perfect?"

"They are good enough as they are. Their stock was cretinous; should we then waste cooperative flesh? Should we kill the cretins and condemn sensitive men to such toil?" The Palasedran's lips curved in a sour smile. "It would be as if we put all our cretins into the upper castes."

"Before we sit down to a ceremonial banquet," said Mialambre, "let me ask this: do you use these creatures for food?"

"There will be no ceremonial banquet."

The carriage rattled along the esplanade, then halted at an inn. The Palasedran made a gesture. "Here you may rest for a period."

Etzwane stared haughtily at the Palasedran. "You bring the envoys of Shant to a waterfront tavern?"

"Where else should we take you? Do you care to pace up and down the esplanade? Should we loft you to the castle of Duke Shaian?"

"We are not sticklers for formality," explained Mialambre. "Still, if you sent envoys to Shant, they would be housed in a splendid palace."

"You accurately represent the distinction between our nations."

Etzwane alighted from the carriage. "Come," he said shortly. "We are not here for pomp and ceremony."

The three marched to the inn. A door of timber planks opened into a narrow room panelled with varnished wood. High along one wall yellow lamps flickered; below were tables and chairs.

An old man with a white shawl over his head stepped forward. "Your wants?"

"A meal and lodging for the night. We are envoys from Shant."

"I will prepare a room. Sit then, and food will be served to you."

The single other occupant of the room, a spare man in a grey cloak, sat at a table with a platter of fish before him. Etzwane stopped short, puzzled by the familiar poise of head. The man looked around, nodded, returned to work fastidiously at his fish.

Etzwane stood indecisively, then went to stand by the man's table. "I thought you had returned to Earth."

"Such were the orders of the Institute," said Ifness. "However I made an urgent protest and I am now on Durdane in a somewhat altered capacity. I am happy to say, moreover, that I have not been expelled from the Institute."

"Good news indeed," said Etzwane. "May we join you?"

"Certainly."

The three took seats. Etzwane performed introductions. "These persons are Patricians of Shant: Mialambre: Octagon and Jerd Finnerack. This gentlemen" – he indicated Ifness – "is an Earthman and Fellow of the Historical Institute. His name is Ifness."

"Precisely true," said Ifness. "I have had an interesting sojourn upon Durdane."

"Why did you not make your presence known?" demanded Etzwane. "You owed a large responsibility to the situation."

Ifness made a gesture of indifference. "Your management of the crisis was not only competent but local. Is it not better that the enemies of Shant fear Shant rather than Earth?"

"The question is many-sided," said Etzwane. "What do you do here in Palasedra?"

"I study the society, which is of great interest. The Palasedrans dare anthromorphological experiments which have few counterparts elsewhere. A frugal people, they adapt human waste material to a set of useful functions. The indefatigable resource of the human spirit is a continuing wonder. In an austere land the Palasedrans have evolved a philosophical system by which they take pleasure in austerity."

Etzwane recognized Ifness' old tendency towards evasive prolixity. "In Garwiy I noticed no tendency of your own towards austerity, nor did you espouse a philosophy glorifying want."

"You observed accurately," said Ifness. "As a scholar I am able to transcend my personal inclinations."

For a brief period Etzwane tried to puzzle out the sense of Ifness' words, then said: "You do not seem to wonder at our presence here in Palasedra."

"A person who conceals his curiosity has knowledge thrust upon him, so I have learned."

"Did you know that the Roguskhoi have sought refuge on Palasedran soil? That our Flyers and the Black Dragons of Palasedra have engaged in combat?"

"This is interesting information," declared Ifness, neglecting a direct answer to the question. "I wonder how the Palasedrans will deal with the Roguskhoi."

Finnerack snorted in disgust. "Do you doubt that the Palasedrans sponsor the Roguskhoi?"

"I do indeed, if only for socio-psychological reasons. Consider the Eagle-Dukes who live in grandeur: are these men to gnaw quietly at the vitals of an enemy? I could not be so convinced."

Finnerack said curtly, "Theorize as you will. What my instincts assert, I believe."

Food was brought to the table: salt fish stewed in vinegar, coarse bread, a pickle of sea fruits. "The Palasedrans have no concept of gastronomy," Ifness noted. "They eat from hunger. Pleasure as defined by a Palasedran is victory over hardship, the assertion of self over environment. The Palasedrans swim at dawn towards the sunrise. When a storm rages they climb a crag. As a secret accomplishment a man may know five phases of mathematics. The Eagle-Dukes build their own towers with stone they quarry with their own hands; some gather their own food. The Palasedrans know no music; one food is as good as another; they adorn themselves only with the emblems of their guarantors. They are neither cordial nor generous, but they are too proud to be suspicious."

Ifness paused to study first Mialambre, then Etzwane, and finally Finnerack. "The Chancellor will presently arrive. I doubt if he will show much sympathy for your problems. If you have no objection I will join your group in the role, let us say, of observer. I have already represented myself as a traveller from Shant."

"As you wish," said Etzwane, despite Finnerack's grunt.

Mialambre: said, "Tell us of the planet Earth, the home of our perverse ancestors."

Ifness pursed his lips. "Earth is not a world briefly to be described. We are perhaps over civilized; our ambitions are no longer large. Our schismatics go forth to the outer worlds; by some miracle we continue to generate adventurers. The human universe constantly expands, and here, if anywhere, is the basic essence of Earth. It is the home world, the source from which all derives."

"Our ancestors left Earth nine thousand years ago," said Mialambre. "They fared through space a vast distance to Durdane, where they thought to be isolated forever. Perhaps now we are no longer remote from other Earth-worlds."

"This is the case," said Ifness. "Durdane still lies beyond the human perimeter, but to no great degree. . . . The Chancellor has arrived. He comes to transact the business of state in this waterfront tavern, and perhaps it is as good a system as any."

The Chancellor stood in the doorway, talking to someone in the street, then he turned and surveyed the room: a man tall and gaunt, with a stubble of grey hair, an enormous crescent of a nose. He wore the usual black gown, but rather than a hat he wore a workman's white shawl about his head.

Etzwane, Finnerack, Mialambre rose to their feet; Ifness sat looking down at the floor as if in sudden reverie.

The Chancellor approached the table. "Please sit down. Our business is simple. Your flyers entered Palasedra; the Black Dragons drove them back. You state that you invaded us to punish the Roguskhoi; these, you further claim, are agents of Palasedra. I say: the Roguskhoi are now on Palasedran soil and Palasedrans shall deal with them. I say: the Roguskhoi are not agents of Palasedra. I say: to send your flyers into Palasedra was a rash and foolish act – indeed, so rash and so foolish that we have held back our hands from sheer astonishment."

Ifness made an approving sign and uttered a somewhat sententious remark, apparently addressed to no one: "Another aspect of human behaviour to confuse and deter our enemies: which is to say, unpredictable forebearance."

The Chancellor frowned aside, not finding in Ifness' approval the exact degree of meek and happy gratitude he might have expected. He spoke more sharply. "I say: we shall disregard your acts, insofar as official and purposeful malice seem to be lacking. In the future you must control your flyers. This, in sum, is my statement. I will now hear your response."

Mialambre cleared his throat. "Our presence here speaks for itself. We hope to foster calm and easy relations between our countries, to our mutual benefit. Ignorance induces suspicion; it is not surprising that some of us saw in the Roguskhoi a renewed threat from Palasedra."

Finnerack spoke in a cold voice: "The Brave Free Men and the Flyers of Shant have defeated the Roguskhoi, who thereupon took purposeful refuge in Palasedra. You assert that the Roguskhoi are not your agents. You do not, however, disclaim responsibility for their existence, you who shamelessly breed men to special uses as if they were cattle; if this is the case, the Roguskhoi remain a Palasedran responsibility. They have done vast damage to Shant, and we demand indemnification."

The Chancellor drew back; he had not expected remarks so energetic, nor, for that matter, had Etzwane and Mialambre. Ifness nodded approvingly. "Finnerack's demands are by all accounts justified, if in fact Palasedran responsibility for the Roguskhoi is real. We have heard no official Palasedran statement either admitting or denying such responsibility."

The Chancellor's grizzled eyebrows became a bar across the bridge of his enormous nose. He spoke to Ifness. "I am puzzled by your exact status in this colloquy."

"I am an independent counsellor," said Ifness. "Gastel Etzwane will endorse my presence, though officially I represent neither Shant nor Palasedra."

The Chancellor said, "It is all the same to me. To make our position absolutely clear, the Palasedrans deny responsibility of any sort whatever for the Roguskhoi."

Finnerack challenged the remark: "Why then do they take refuge in Palasedra? Where did they come from if not Palasedra?"

The Chancellor spoke in a measured voice: "Our most recent intelligence is this: they are creatures sent here from the planet Earth. A spaceship discharged them into the Engh, a remote valley not far from the Salt Bog." Etzwane turned to stare at Ifness, who looked blandly at the far wall. Finnerack uttered a harsh bark of laughter. The Chancellor went on: "So much we have learned from ahulphs of the neighbourhood. The Roguskhoi now return to the Engh. They will not arrive; a force of Palasedran warriors goes now to destroy them. Tomorrow I go to witness the battle and collect further information; accompany me, if you wish."

CHAPTER FIFTEEN

The Chancellor laid a map upon the table and gestured out into the predawn murk. "There is the Engh. From here it appears no more than a defile or a gully. The mountains in fact enclose a large, barren meadow, as is evident from the map." The Chancellor tapped a horny finger-nail down upon the parchment. "The glider discharged us here; we now stand at this point, overlooking the valley of the River Zek. Troops deploy in yonder forest; they will presently move forward."

"And what of the Roguskhoi?" asked Etzwane.

"The main force has left the Great Salt Bog and now approaches. The prodromes have already entered the Engh, which we have not disturbed." He peered into the dawn sky. "There is no wind to support the Black Dragons; our reconnaissance is incomplete. As yet I have not been informed of battle plans."

The three suns rolled up into the sky; violet light flooded the valley; the river Zek showed a series of col-oured glints. Finnerack pointed to the north. "Here come the advance parties. Why do you not harass them on the flank?"

"I am not battle-chief," said the Chancellor. "I can

211

supply no opinion. . . . Stand back so that we cannot be observed."

Scout parties jogged up the valley; in the distance a dark mass advanced like a tidal bore.

An instrument at the Chancellor's belt tinkled. He held it to his ear and presently scanned the sky. He returned the instrument to his belt.

The Roguskhoi approached in hulking, long strides, features fixed and blank. To the side jogged the chieftains, distinguished by their pectoral bibs of chain mail.

The Chancellor's belt radio jingled; he listened with stern attention, then said, "No alteration of plan."

He returned the radio to his belt and stood a moment looking silently towards the Engh. He said, "Last night the spaceship returned to the Engh. It waits there now, for purposes open to conjecture."

Mialambre spoke sardonically to Ifness. "Can you suggest an explanation for this?"

"Yes," said the Ifness. "I can indeed." He asked the Chancellor: "What is the semblance of the spaceship? Have men disembarked? What is its insignia, if any?"

"I learn that the ship is a great round disc. The ports lay open, making ramps to the ground. No one has left the ship. Skirmishers now attack the rear of the column."

An irregular rattle of explosions reached their ears. The Roguskhoi chieftains swung about, then uttered sharp orders; groaning and rumbling, the Roguskhoi broke apart to form battle squads. The length of the column was now visible. Full-grown warriors marched at front and rear; in the centre were imps, bantlings, and perhaps a hundred dazed and haggard women.

From the forest came the blast of a horn; the Palasedran troops moved deliberately forth.

Etzwane was perplexed. He had expected gigantic warriors to match the Roguskhoi bulk for bulk; the Palasedran troops were not as tall as himself, but immensely broad of shoulder and deep of chest, with arms dangling almost to the ground. The heads hunched low, the eyes peered from under black helmets, seeming to look in two directions. They wore ochre trousers, fibre epaulettes, and greaves; for weapons they carried sabres, short-handled axes, small shields, and dart guns.

The Palesedrans bounded forward at a trot. The Roguskhoi halted, taken aback. The chieftains bawled commands, the squads reformed. The Palasedrans halted; the two armies faced each other, a hundred yards apart.

"A curious confrontation, to be sure," mused Ifness. "Each solution to the problem offers advantages.... Hmmm. Ogres versus trolls. The weapons I judge equivalent. Tactics and agility, of course, must decide the issue."

The Roguskhoi chieftains called sudden, harsh orders; abandoning women and imps the Roguskhoi warriors ran at a lumbering trot for the Engh. The Palasedrans ran on a converging course, and the armies came together, not face to face, but side to side, the Roguskhoi hacking and slicing, the Palasedrans bounding in and out, chopping, occasionally shooting darts at Roguskhoi eyes, and when occasion offered, tackling the legs of a vulnerable Roguskhoi, to bring the maroon bulk toppling. The scimitars took a corresponding toll; the way became littered with arms, legs, heads, and torsos; red blood mingled with black.

The battle reached the mouth of the Engh; and here a second Palasedran army bounded down from the rocks. The Roguskhoi thrust forward, striving to enter the Engh by dint of sheer strength. Behind in the valley remained the women and imps. The women became prey to hysteria. They picked up discarded weapons and slashed at the hopping imps, screaming in maniac delight.

The Roguskhoi warriors had gained the floor of the Engh. Here, with room for their agility, the Palasedrans became more effective.

Finnerack first, with Ifness and Etzwane close behind, then Mialambre and the Chancellor, came over a low, wooded ridge and looked down into the Engh, an irregular flat area about a half-mile in diameter, carpeted with scrub and blue rockweed. At the centre rested the spaceship: a flattened hemisphere of brown metal two hundred feet in diameter.

Etzwane asked Ifness, "What sort is the spaceship?"

"I don't know." Ifness brought forth his camera and made a series of photographs.

On three sides segments of the hull hung open. Standing in the apertures were creatures Etzwane thought to be either andromorphs or men; in the shadows he could not be certain.

In the Engh the battle raged, the Roguskhoi step by step thrusting towards the spaceship, the bibbed chieftains in the van, the rank and file arranged in such a fashion as to protect them from the bounding Palasedrans.

Finnerack gave a grunt of anguish and started down the hill. "Finnerack!" cried Etzwane. "Where are you going?"

Finnerack paid no heed. He broke into a trot. Etzwane set off after him. "Finnerack! Come back here; are you mad?"

Finnerack ran, waving his arms towards the spaceship. His eyes bulged wide-open, but he did not appear to see;

he stumbled, and Etzwane was on him. Etzwane clutched Finnerack's waist, pulled back. "What are you doing?" Have you gone insane?"

Finnerack groaned, kicked, fought; he drove his elbows into Etzwane's face.

Ifness stepped forward and struck two smart blows; Finnerack fell numbly back.

"Quick, or they'll kill us from the ship," said Ifness.

Mialambre and Ifness took Finnerack's arms, Etzwane his legs; they carried him back into the shelter of the trees. Using Finnerack's garments, Ifness tied his ankles and wrists.

In the Engh the Palasedrans, wary of the spaceship, drew back. Up the ramps marched the surviving Roguskhoi chieftains and a hundred warriors. The ports snapped shut. Like a glow-beetle, the ship took on a silver luminescence. Emitting a rasping squeal it rose into the sky and presently was gone.

The Roguskhoi remaining in the valley moved slowly to the spot where the spaceship had rested; here they formed a rough circle, to stand at bay. The chieftains had departed; of the copper horde which had almost overwhelmed Shant less than a thousand survived.

The Palasedrans, drawing back, formed a pair of lines to the right and left of the Roguskhoi; they stood quietly, awaiting orders. For ten minutes the armies surveyed each other soberly, without signal of hostility; then the Palasedrans withdrew to the edge of the Engh and retired up the slope. The Roguskhoi remained at the centre of the valley.

The Chancellor made a signal to the men of Shant. "We now adopt our original strategy. The Roguskhoi are sealed into the Engh and they will never escape. Even your blue-eyed madman must concede the Roguskhoi to be off-world creatures."

Ifness said, "As to this there was never any doubt. The purpose for the incursion remains a mystery. If a conventional conquest were the plan, why were the Roguskhoi armed only with scimitars? Can folk who fly space contrive no better weapons? It seems unreasonable on the face of the matter."

"Evidently they took us lightly," said the Chancellor. "Or perhaps they thought to test us. If so, we have dealt them harsh instruction."

"These conjectures are reasonable," Ifness said. "There is still much to be learned. Certain of the Roguskhoi chieftains were killed. I suggest that you convey these corpses to one of your medical laboratories and there perform investigations, in which I would wish to participate."

The Chancellor made a curt gesture. "The effort is unnecessary."

Ifness drew the Chancellor aside and spoke a few calm sentences, and now the Chancellor gave grudging agreement to Ifness' proposals.

CHAPTER SIXTEEN

In a state of sullen apathy Finnerack marched back down the valley. Several times Etzwane started to speak to him; each time, eery and sick at heart, he held his tongue. Mialambre, less imaginative, asked Finnerack: "Do you realize that your act, sane or the reverse, imperilled us all?"

Finnerack made no response; Etzwane wondered if he even heard.

Ifness said in a grave voice, "The best of us at times act upon odd impulses."

Finnerack said nothing.

Etzwane had expected to be flown back across the Great Salt Bog; the black glider, however, took them south to Chemaoue, where the man-powered carriage conveyed them once again to the dour inn at the harbour. The chambers were as cheerless as the refectory, with couches of stone cushioned only by thin, sour-smelling pads. Through the open window came a draught of cool salt air and the sound of harbour water.

Etzwane passed a cheerless night, during which he was not aware of having slept. Grey-violet light finally entered the high window. Etzwane arose, rinsed his face with cold water, and went down to the common room, where he was presently joined by Mialambre. Ifness and Finnerack failed to appear. When Etzwane went to investigate, he found their chambers vacant.

At noon Ifness returned to the inn. Etzwane anxiously inquired in regard to Finnerack. Ifness replied with care and deliberation. "Finnerack, if you remember, displayed a peculiar irresponsibility. Last night he departed the inn and set off along the shore. I had anticipated something of the sort and asked that he be kept under surveillance. Last night, therefore, he was taken into custody. I have been with the Palasedran authorities all morning and they have, I believe, discovered the source of Finnerack's odd conduct."

The rancour which Etzwane had once felt in connection with the secretive Ifness began to return. "What did they find out – and how?"

"Best perhaps that you come with me and see for yourself."

Ifness spoke in a casual voice: "The Palasedrans are now convinced that the spaceship is not a product of Earth. I naturally could have told them as much, in the process betraying my own background."

Mialambre asked irritably. "Where then did the spaceship originate?"

"I am as anxious to learn this as yourself – in fact I work on Durdane to this end. Since the Earth-worlds lie beyond the Schiafarilla, the spaceship presumably comes from the general direction opposite, towards the centre of the galaxy. It is a sort I have never seen before."

"You informed the Palasedrans of all this?"

"By no means. Their opinions were altered by this morning's events. The Roguskhoi chieftains, if you recall,

218

wore a protective bib; this aroused my curiosity. . . . Here are the laboratories."

Etzwane felt a thrill of horror. "This is where they brought Finnerack?"

"It seemed a sensible procedure."

They entered a building of black stone smelling strongly of chemical reeks. Ifness led the way with assurance along a side corridor into a large chamber illuminated by an array of skylights. Tanks and vats stood to right and left; tables ran down the middle. At the far end four Palasedrans in grey smocks considered the bulk of a dead Roguskhoi. Ifness gave a nod of approval. "They commence a new investigation. . . . It may be profitable for you to watch."

Etzwane and Mialambre approached and stood by the wall. The Palasedrans worked without haste, arranging the hulk to best advantge. . . . Etzwane looked about the room. A pair of large brown insects or crustaceans moved inside two glass jars. Glass tanks displayed floating organs, moulds and fungus, a swarm of small white worms, a dozen unnameable objects. . . . The Palasedrans, using an air-driven circular saw, sliced into the great chest. . . . They worked five minutes with great dexterity. Etzwane began to feel an almost unbearable tension; he turned away. Ifness however was intent. "Now watch."

With deftness and delicacy the Palasedrans extracted a white sac the size of two clenched fists. A pair of heavy, trailing tendons or nerves appeared to lead up into the neck. The Palasedrans carefully cut channels into the dark flesh, through bone and cartilage, to draw forth the cords intact. The entire organ now lay on the table. Suddenly it evinced a squirming life of its own. The white sac broke away; out crawled a glossy brown creature, something between a spider and a crab. The Palasedrans at once clapped it into a bottle and placed it on the shelf beside its two fellows.

"There you see your true enemy," said Ifness. "Sajarano of Sershan, during our conversations, used the word 'asutra.' Its intelligence appears to be of the highest order."

In horrified fascination Etzwane went to stare into the bottle. The creature was gnarled and convoluted like a small brown brain; eight jointed legs left the underside of the body, each terminating in three strong little palps. The long fibres or nerves extended from one end through a cluster of sensory organs.

"From my brief acquaintance with the asutra," said Ifness, "I deduce it to be a parasite; or better perhaps, the directive half of a symbiosis, though I am certain that in its native environment it uses neither creatures like the Roguskhoi nor yet men for its hosts."

Etzwane spoke in a voice he found hard to control. "You have seen these before?"

"A single specimen only: that which I took from Sajarano."

A dozen questions pushed into Etzwane's mind: grisly suspicions he did not know how to voice and perhaps did not wish verified. He put Sajarano of Sershan and his pathetic, mangled corpse out of his mind. He looked from one bottle to the other, and though he could not identify eyes or visual organs he had the disturbing sense of scrutiny.

"They are highly evolved and specialized," stated Ifness. "Still, like man they exhibit a surprising hardihood and no doubt can survive even in the absence of their hosts."

Etzwane asked: "What then of Finnerack?" – although he knew the answer to the question even before he asked.

"This," said Ifness, tapping one of the bottles, "was the asutra which occupied the body of Jerd Finnerack."

"He is dead?"

"He is dead. How could he be alive?"

"Once again," said Ifness in a nasal voice of intense boredom, "you insist that I render you information regarding matters either not essentially your concern, or which you might ascertain independently. Still, I will in this case make a concession and perhaps ease your agonies of bewilderment.

"As you know, I was ordered off the plant Durdane by representatives of the Historical Institute, who felt that I had acted irresponsibly. I forcefully asserted my opinions; I won others to my point of view and was sent back to Durdane in a new capacity.

"I returned at once to Garwiy, where I satisfied myself that you had acted with energy and decision. In short, the men of Shant, given leadership, reacted to the threat with ordinary human resource."

"But why the Roguskhoi in the first place? Why should they attack the folk of Shant? Is it not extraordinary?"

"By no means. Durdane is an isolated world of men, where experiments with human populations can be discreetly performed. The asutra appear to be anticipating an eventual contact between their realm and the Earthworlds; perhaps they have had unhappy experiences in the past.

"Remember, they are parasites; they will try to effect their aims through proxies. First, then, they attempt an anti-human simulacrum which impregnates human females and in the process renders them sterile: a biological weapon, in fact, which man has often used against insect pests.

"Their remarkable creation is the Roguskhoi. Certainly hundreds, perhaps thousands of men and women have known the asutra laboratories: a thought to haunt your dark nights. The asutra must consider their creatures acceptable human replicas, which of course they are not; the more subtle human gaze recognizes them for monsters at once; still, biologically they fulfil their function.

"To insure a meaningful experiment, the Roguskhoi must be accorded a period of non-interference; hence the Anome has a monitor implanted in his body, and his Benevolences fare no better. By a system not at all clear the asutra control the activities of their hosts. Sajarano complained of his 'secret soul,' 'the voice of his soul'; I recall Finnerack mentioning his conscience. No doubt the asutra learned to admonish men in their laboratories.

"The Roguskhoi, as weapons, were faulty; the essential concept was a fallacy. Once the artificial passivity of the Anome had ended, the men of Shant reacted with ordinary human energy. No doubt the asutra could have supplied weapons and subjugated Shant, but this was not their purpose; they wished to test and perfect indirect techniques.

"Suppose the men could be induced to destroy each other? This concept, or so I suspect – here I am on uncertain ground – led to the planting of a control in Finnerack. His pugnacity was reinforced; he was compelled to challenge the Palasedrans – an act not at all contrary to his own instincts.

"This second experiment likewise led to failure, although in principle it seems a more reasonable tactic. There was insufficient preparation; I suspect the scheme to be a hasty improvisation."

"All very well," said Mialambre with a scowl, "but why should Finnerack be used rather than, say, Gastel Etzwane, who has always wielded more real influence?"

"At one time Finnerack looked to be a man of irresistible power," said Ifness. "He controlled the Intelligence Agency and also commanded the Brave Free Men. His star was on the rise, and so he certified his doom."

"This is the case,"admitted Mialambre. "In fact, I can fix upon the precise time of his alteration. He disappeared for three days. . . ." His voice dwindled; his eyes shifted towards Etzwane.

A heavy silence came over the chamber.

Etzwane brought his clenched fists slowly down on the table. "So it must be. The asutra have altered me as well."

"Interesting!" remarked Ifness. "You are conscious of strange voices, agonizing pangs, a constant sense of discontent and unease? These were the symptoms which eventually drove Sajarano to suicide."

"I know none of these. Nevertheless I was drugged precisely as was Finnerack. The same Parthans were on hand. I am doomed, but I die with my goals achieved. Let us go to the laboratory and have an end to the business."

Ifness made a reassuring sign. "Conditions are not so bad as you fear. I suspected that such an effort might be made upon you, and was on hand to thwart the attempt. In fact, I occupied a suite in the Hrindiana precisely beside your own. The attempt failed; the Parthans died; the asutra went to Earth in a jar and you awoke three days later tired and bewildered, but none the worse for all that."

Etzwane sank back into his seat.

Ifness continued, "In Shant the asutra have suffered a small but significant defeat. Their experiments have gained them precisely that attention they sought to avoid, thanks to the alertness of the Historical Institute. What have we learned? That the asutra either expect or prepare for antagonistic relations with the human race. Perhaps a collision between a pair of expanding world-systems is at last imminent. . . . Here comes the Chancellor, no doubt to announce that your glider is ready. As for me, I have eaten salt fish once too often, and if you permit, I will accompany you to Shant. . . ."